Spark

Smoke and Moonlight: Book 1

By

A.M. Burns

See what A.M. Burns is up to.
Visit his website www.amburns.com
Sign up for his email list

Copyright 2020 © MysticHawker Press

http://www.mystichawker.com/

ISBN: 978-1-945632-88-4

Edited by Robert Brownson
Cover art by Silver Circle Images

Other Books by A.M. Burns

Shifter Force
1: Visions of Rage
2: Visions of Shadows
3: Visions of Stars

Yellow Sky Coven:
1: Blood Moon Yellow Sky
2: Dark Stars of Dallas

Stand Alone Books:
The Black Fin Case

YA Books:
Coyote's Pup

Familiar Series:
1: Familiar Path
2: Familiar Spirit

Books in the Infragilis Universe.

Solstice Properties Mysteries
1: Second Story Hex
2: Watchtower WooWoo
3: Mid-Century Monster

Tempest Academy Prologue
Running in a Pack
Into the Sky
Shifting Tides

SPARK

Other Books by A.M. Burns

Shifter Force
1: Visions of Rage
2: Visions of Shadows
3: Visions of Stars

Yellow Sky Coven:
1: Blood Moon Yellow Sky
2: Dark Stars of Dallas

Stand Alone Books:
The Black Fin Case

YA Books:
Coyote's Pup

Familiar Series:
1: Familiar Path
2: Familiar Spirit

Books in the Infragilis Universe.

Solstice Properties Mysteries
1: Second Story Hex
2: Watchtower WooWoo
3: Mid-Century Monster

Tempest Academy Prologue
Running in a Pack
Into the Sky
Shifting Tides

1

The dust blocked out the ever-present sun as the wind whipped around me. The tiny shards of sand bit into my face. I jerked up my dust mask and pulled down the brim of my Kevlar helmet. Even the bulk of the two Hummers the unit had been in wasn't enough to stifle the wind and sand in the least. Somehow, I doubted the attack on us coming seconds before a sandstorm was a coincidence. For almost two weeks, our satellite connection had been broken. Since then, it had been one storm after another. Our best hope was that the insurgents would be as blinded as we were. We had no hope of getting the Hummers going again until the storm broke, but we could use them as landmarks.

A slight burst of static sounded though my helmet radio. "Move away from the Hummers, keep from being easier targets. We don't want to cluster together, waiting to be picked off."

Following orders, I took off a few steps before the radio sounded again. The short-range communications were the best we could hope for since we couldn't connect to the wider systems. Even GPS was unreliable. None of it made sense. Technology had become unreliable.

"Hunker down!" The words came through my helmet radio. The thing I wanted to ask our platoon sergeant was where we were supposed to hunker down. Sandstorms were nothing new, but the way they kept coming out of nowhere; it was like they were alive, rising out of the desert without warning and swarming over us. We were hardened US Army Rangers, but something in the Afghan wilds had been harrowing us for months and after losing more than half our unit to a pack of werewolves, the sands themselves seemed to be against us as we struggled to get back to base.

"Something's got me!" Carson's voice rang out in my radio.

"I'm coming." I jerked around. Right before the storm closed over us, Carson had been a few feet from me. Hidden in the gritty grayness, he wasn't visible, but the smell of his cigarettes was enough. The man was a chain smoker and the reek of nicotine clung to him so strongly, it even covered the awful aftershave he used.

After a couple of steps in his direction, the wind pushed against me harder. It felt like the wind knew I was trying to save him and was determined to keep me away. With each step, the gale-force shoved me back. It was all I could do to force my feet free of the sands that clung to me like some kind of mud or tar.

Carson screamed. The sound carried through the air and the radio.

"Carson. What's wrong?" Sergeant First Class Dern had been on the other side of the dune before the sandstorm settled on us. He sounded frantic. None of us had signed on for any of the things we'd dealt with over the past month.

Gritting my teeth, as the sand seeped around my dust mask and the dune felt like it was trying to crawl up my legs, I pulled my foot free of the dirt and took another step. Something inside me growled. Since I didn't have my mic pressed, the sound shouldn't have carried over the radio. I hoped it didn't.

For a second, the pressure of the wind and sand around me paused. It was like the growl had scared it. But a sandstorm wasn't alive or at least wasn't supposed to be. And things like werewolves weren't supposed to exist either. However, nothing was going to be able to remove the sight of half of my unit being torn to shreds by the huge furry creatures that had savaged us while a full moon hung above us. Even machine gun fire hadn't been enough to stop them. If they could be real, what other secrets did the desert hide?

"Hang on, Carson." I managed to get three steps closer. It should've been enough. He hadn't been far away.

The sand hit me harder than before.

I staggered backward. "Damn it." How did I fight a sandstorm? Where was Carson?

A huge gust of wind caught me and lifted me free of the dune, wrenching my rifle away. It slammed me down hard on my face.

On my hands and knees, I crept forward. There was no sign of my rifle.

Deep inside me, where the growl had come from, it felt natural to be on all fours. I let my helmet take the brunt of the wind's assault and forced myself to keep heading to where I'd last seen Carson.

The sands curled around me but stayed just shy of touching. I still couldn't see more than a few inches, but it was easier to close the distance to where the pack of cigarettes lay mostly covered in gray sand.

Hitting the mic button on my chest, I shouted. "Carson! Where are you?"

The winds answered me with relentless howls.

"Lucas, report." Dern's voice didn't carry well through the wind chattering over the mics. "Where's Carson?" Sergeant Dern sounded frantic in a way I'd never heard before. Even when we'd been attacked by the werewolves, he'd never broken. The lack of communication with base hadn't phased him, he'd just kept us moving. Previous storms hadn't shaken him, but there was something different about this storm.

"I've got his smokes, but not him."

Something brushed my shoulder.

Spinning as fast as I could on hands and knees, I tried to see what it was, but the storm swallowed it before I could make anything out.

A huge heavy force caught me in the side, knocking me over. I rolled down a slope that shouldn't have been there. Darkness beyond the sandstorm engulfed me. The winds died down and the smell of nicotine was all around.

"Carson, sound off." I didn't know where I was. I reached back and pulled my flashlight from its loop on my backpack. It would really suck if the sand had gotten into the batteries and messed with the contacts.

I flipped it on.

At my feet, Carson lay, or his head did. The rest of him was a yard or so away, barely visible in the light's beam.

I yanked my revolver from the holster at my hip.

Above us, the storm raged.

Panning the light around the room, I kept the Sig Sauer pointed at the center of the flashlight's beam. Adrenaline surged through me. Another growl rumbled out of me. Carson had been a member of my unit for two years, time we had spent ranging through the desert, stopping terrorists before they had a chance to finish their training and go places where they could cause damage. We were an elite squad, one of the best, and he lay in pieces in the sand. I wanted to kill whatever had taken him out.

As the light passed over a pile of rocks a few feet away, something moved in the shadows. Reflexively I squeezed the trigger. The Sig barked sharply once. I didn't want to scare off whatever it was. I wanted to kill it.

The shadows entered the flashlight beam. Tendrils of darkness snaked toward me. I fired again, three rounds. Two pinged off rocks I couldn't see, but one hit something soft. If I could hit it, I could kill it.

Deep inside me, the idea of killing what was stalking me made me growl again. The sound focused me, and the tendrils stood out from the ambient darkness of the chamber I stood in. I squinted and focused. There was a definite difference between the tendrils and the shadows. A human silhouette seemed to be at the middle of the tendrils. The next growl helped me aim. I got off another shot, tight into the center of the silhouette. With a high-pitched scream that made me want to cover my ears, the grasping, shadowed arms retreated.

I fired again.

Another scream rewarded me, right before a tendril caught me in the gut, hurling me back several feet, into a hard wall. My sig slipped out of my hand. Pain shot through my back, and I dropped a couple of feet, but somehow managed to stay upright.

"Damn it." I fumbled desperately not to drop the flashlight.

The screaming had ended, but I couldn't see the source anymore. The rest of the chamber was clear, only slightly dimmer than regular light as I glanced around for my target. Something moved across the pile of stones I'd spotted earlier. The rocks appeared to have been placed there, not just fallen. Dust and shadows fought for supremacy there. It made it hard to make out details.

"Sergeant Dern, Carson and I fell in a hole of some sort." I rattled everything off as the shadows moved like an octopus across the rocks. The central human shape was gone. "There's something else down here. It got Carson."

Silence rewarded my effort to report in.

Cold wind rushed down into the chamber, bringing more dirt and sand with it.

I blinked back the grit.

Another shape moved in the dust. It wasn't exactly light, but it glowed softly and the shadows retreated from it as it hadn't from my flashlight beam.

Keeping my gaze on the light and shadow as they began a strange dance that was like two lovers determined to touch, yet terrified at the prospect, I knelt and felt around for my pistol. Somehow I doubted either of the two knives I carried would do any real damage to either the light or the shadow.

The pistol lay in the dirt, just the tip of the barrel sticking out.

"Damn it." Gritting my teeth, I pulled the pistol up. I rarely carried a spare pistol, too much a chance of enemy combatants taking one away and using it on me or one of my unit, plus I wasn't great at firing two pistols at once. The right hand was always slightly off when I did that.

The light lunged at the darkness like some kind of spear. It impaled one of the tendrils.

Another shriek reverberated through the chamber. The sound was so much higher. Reflexively, I put my fingers in my ears. My pistol fell again, as did the flashlight.

The light blazed so bright that I didn't need my own source of illumination at that moment, but I wanted my gun.

Another darkness launched itself from behind the pile of stones. It engulfed the light and the first darkness rushed out of the chamber, brushing past me in a cold wind.

I dropped to my knees as the shrieking stopped. Frantically I dared to glance away from the light and shadows lost in a battle that I was sure was going to end in my death. Even the werewolves we'd fought had been flesh and blood. These things were something totally different. They had to be spirits, something the friendly locals were always going on about.

When the light pulsed hard, the shadow fell back across the rocks.

I found my pistol and jerked it up. For a second, I had a clear line of sight and took the shot.

The sig clicked.

"Son of a bitch." I slid the chamber open and shook it. Sand fell out along with the next bullet in the chamber. The last bullet. I didn't have time to reload. I threw the empty chunk of metal across the chamber toward the darkness before pulling out both of my knives and following it.

A smile welled up inside me. Rushing across the chamber toward the darkness with just my knives felt good. My claws had finally come out and blood, or whatever was inside that shadow, was going to stain the sands.

A tendril batted the sig away. It hit the wall with a solid thud, telling me it was never going to fire again.

The light flared and hit the shadows where they lay across the rocks.

Shimmering, as if in pain, the tendril lashed out at the light as I slashed at the darkness.

We three collided. I roared like an animal as I stabbed the shadow so deeply that my blade hit the altar rocks under it hard enough to jar the knife from my grasp. There was so much resistance to my attack that I couldn't help but bare my teeth. Even if it killed me, I had scored a hit. I was going to die as a warrior.

That's all that mattered.

Somewhere a bell rang. It was a light chime, almost like the bells some belly dancers wore in old films. But it was different. It made every hair on my body stand on end. The ferocity that had been roaring out of me subsided in an instant, before the chime even ended.

The light flared in that moment.

All the shadows were blasted into fragments that slowly faded as the light dimmed.

Something warm touched my hand.

"She likes you. Take care of her."

The light blinked out, like it had never been there.

A cool metallic shape rested in my palm. To avoid dropping it, I slipped it into my pocket. I needed to find my flashlight.

Carefully, I shuffled my feet across the chamber. Several yards from the pile of rocks, nearly to the far wall, I kicked something. Bending down, I retrieved the flashlight and my sidearm, happy to have the familiar weights in my hand again. It wasn't much, but if someone came at me, I could beat them.

I needed to get out of the chamber and see what had happened to my unit. The winds above the hole had died down and no fresh sand was pouring in around me.

Hitting the mic button, I stared up at the sky that was slowly returning to its unrelenting blue. The sun blazed just shy of the edge of the hole I'd fallen into. There should be someone up there. The storm couldn't have killed them all. "Sergeant Dern, this is

Sergeant Lucas. I could use a hand here."

Letting go of the button, I waited for a response. There was nothing.

The sand had piled high enough to give me a slight incline to crawl up. Sand could be slippery and dangerous. After trying to scramble up it on my feet, and then on my hands and knees, I finally had to lie down and almost swim along its ever-shifting surface to reach the dune we'd been standing on when the sand storm hit.

Blinking back the bright light, I turned, slowly taking in the scene around me. The buried bulk of the hummers were the only thing defined, but nothing moved. Everything was completely still, with not even a whisper of a breeze to move the sands. It felt more like a tomb than the chamber I'd just crawled out of.

2

I frowned as I trudged down the hall of the admin building in Kabul. It had the same feeling as any other army building I'd ever been in. The same utilitarian gray walls and vinyl flooring that was just hard enough to have my boot falls echo ever so slightly. There weren't as many people in the halls as there normally were. It made me wonder if something was going on. Were the rest of the forces deployed in the area having the same problems my unit had encountered or was there an offensive happening I hadn't gotten the intel on? Years before, I'd learned everything in the army was on a need-to-know basis. With the rest of my unit lost in the sandstorm, and whatever the shadows and light had been, most of my sources of intel were gone.

Everyone who'd been part of my life for the past three years was gone. I'd been trying for days, since I'd been rescued, to jump through the hoops of debriefings and paperwork. There was always more paperwork or another request for more information. Even if I wasn't the only one to go over things, it would've been overwhelming. At first, nobody believed me, and then when they did, things got scary. The base commander hadn't batted an eye at what I told him. But he had asked me to not talk about it and that a specialist would be there soon to talk to me.

Stopping outside a door that looked like every other door in the hall, I glanced at the number on the wall, yeah, it was where I'd been told to go. A knot wrapped around my stomach. When I'd been told that I had to talk to a specialist, I had no idea what to expect. Reflexively, I slipped my hand into my pocket and touched the small silver bell there. The thing the being of light had given me. It might have saved me in the chamber. So far, I hadn't told anyone about it. Although I didn't know what it was, or what it meant, there was something important about it, and I wanted to discover that on my own. The only thing I knew for sure was that it was heavier than it should've been. Like there was something inside, but as far as I could tell, there was just the small ball that gave it its chime.

Letting go of the bell, I knocked on the door before pushing it open.

A tall, dark man in a suit that was just a few shades darker than his skin looked up and smiled. "Sergeant David Lucas, please come in." He waved me to a seat.

There were a couple of old metal chairs on my side of the desk. I went for the one on the left.

"I'm agent Briar, with the FBI."

On reflex, my eyes widened. "Why are the feds involved in this? Aren't we still on foreign soil?" Things were getting stranger and stranger, and I wasn't overly fond of strange. I liked my world nice and straightforward, but lately straightforward had flown right out the window, so I shouldn't have been overly surprised when more strangeness showed up sitting across a desk from me.

Briar let out a long breath. "That's complicated, and I'll explain all of it once we get a few preliminary things out of the way." He took a deep breath, almost like he was smelling a delectable cup of coffee.

He tapped the thick file in front of him. "Sergeant Lucas, it looks like you've been a model soldier. I had one of my people run several searches on you, couldn't find a single blemish on your records, both military and civilian. Does that sound right?"

"Yeah, sounds right." The knot in my stomach tightened harder. There was more to Agent Briar than just FBI, I just couldn't put my finger on it.

"It looks like you basically skipped your way through Ranger training like it was a walk in the park. Your trainers had nothing but good things to say about you."

The knot seized. "Yeah."

Briar nodded. "Report says three weeks ago your unit got attacked by werewolves." The words flowed out smooth as silk.

He was FBI, not a guy with a straight jacket, but the way he looked at me hit me hard. There was something dangerous behind his eyes. The short hair on my neck stood out. "That's right." I wished I still had my sidearm or even one of my knives. Briar was dangerous.

"But it looks like you returned to base too late to administer the antidote."

The word came out of left field. "Antidote? Antidote for what?"

"Lycanthropy." Again, he said something strange like it was a word he used every day and it didn't even bother him.

"Wait a minute. What are you talking about?" Even as I asked, I touched my left arm. After the fight with the werewolves, like most of the guys who lived, I'd had a chunk torn out. The field doctors in the next village over had patched us up, then the next day the wounds were healed when we went to change the bandages.

"Your record and your reaction show that your bite was received on the left leg. Sergeant, have you ever seen a wound heal as fast as the bite the werewolf gave you?"

"But everyone else's bites healed too." My head started pounding. There was something more to it. My hearing had been overly sensitive. Carson's smokes had been harsher than ever. I'd been able to see in that chamber.

"And if they were all still alive, I'd be talking to them too." Briar shook his head, and then rubbed his temple. "Hell, if we were anywhere civilized, we wouldn't be having this conversation. You would've come into the base medic, as soon as the chief medical officer saw what had happened, antidotes would've been given and all memory of a werewolf attack would've been substituted by terrorists or gang members, depending on what matched the town you were in. But you got bitten over a hundred miles outside of Kabul, where nobody knew what you'd really gone up against and didn't know how to respond."

My head swam as I struggled to put the pieces together. "Wait. So, you're trying to tell me I'm now a werewolf?"

"Yeah, that's what I'm telling you. This would be a lot easier if your unit had survived. Hell, I know Washington's been wanting a unit of trained specialist werewolves for a while, but we're doing what we can to stop them from doing it by force. I won't have super-soldiers created under my watch." Briar tapped the desk, the first sign of agitation he'd shown since I entered the room.

I was good at reading people, and Agent Briar was used to being in control. Of himself, of others, he was a major alpha male. Deep inside me, that part that had begun stirring when I'd been in that chamber under the dune stirred and it wanted to roll over and not upset Briar. That was something I wasn't about to do. He had to prove himself to me. Even if he was right and I was a werewolf, I wasn't going to just start acting all submissive to other wolves. It wasn't how I was wired.

"Why haven't they sidestepped you and the FBI and done it anyway?" I didn't want to irritate him, but it was useful intel. Something told me all the intel I could get was going to prove helpful in navigating the minefield I was suddenly standing in.

"Old agreements. Trust me, the people in power keep trying to find ways around them, but someone really powerful and insightful crafted the agreements between us and them."

His phrasing left me wondering where each of us stood.

"If your encounter with the werewolves had happened elsewhere, things would be different. But it didn't." Briar pursed his lips and shook his head. "We'd heard rumors of a new group of supernaturals acting here in the Middle East. I'd hoped they were wrong. Someone or something very powerful is up to no good, or at least no good for American interests."

"Sounds like you need boots on the ground here." There was a split second there that I almost offered to lend them a hand. The werewolves and shadow thing had taken my unit. I owed them blood.

Briar shook his head again, a little more forcefully than the first time. "No way. Sorry, Sergeant, but for the next six months or so, you're a danger to yourself and those around you." He pulled out an official paper from the folder. "This is your DD Two Fourteen."

Somehow the paper sitting there on the desk hit harder than any of his words, or accusations.

"It's not time for that." I shook my head. "I just re-upped two years ago for another four years."

"Honorable medical discharge." Agent Briar pulled out a pen and laid it on the paper. "Part of the ancient agreement between the supernaturals and the US government…legitimate world governments, was that no supernaturals can be part of any branch of the military, either historic or futuristic."

The words sounded so strange and caught me as funny. "So, you're not going to let werewolves go to the moon?"

A soft grin turned up the corners of Briar's mouth. "Not while enlisted. What you do when you get out is up to you. I doubt any of us are going to be able to afford it anytime soon. We also have no idea what would happen to the magic that's part of us when we leave the planet. Magic is complicated."

"Is that what those shadow and light things were, magic?"

"We don't know." He tapped the folder again. "I read your description and I have to say, I've never heard of, or seen anything like it. I've got people researching the description. One of my highest witches says it sounds like some kind of djinn or deva, but she's not sure. Trust me, I'm digging for information, and once I find what I'm looking for, I'll figure out how to deal with it."

"If I'm not a danger anymore when that happens, I want in." I stared at the discharge papers and pen. There was no way I was just going to be kicked to the curb when it came time to give some payback for my unit.

Briar stared at me for a minute or more. My request hung heavy in the air between us. He let out a breath. "You're strong. I can see that. We won't know about your wolf for a while. Our bonding with our wolves can get complicated, as we're not always evenly matched."

"Our wolves," I repeated to him. "So, you're a werewolf? Yes or no is fine." For years I'd followed orders, often without questioning. Maybe if I had raised a few more questions, my company would still be alive. It wasn't fair that I lived and they hadn't.

"Yes." Briar's nod was so slight, I almost missed it. "If your wolf is as strong as you are, if we get a solid lead, and… and I do mean *and*, you gain control of your wolf, I'll consider letting you in."

Leaning back in the chair, I let out a satisfied sigh. "Good. I'll do my best."

"I have no doubt." Again, Briar tapped the folder. "Is there anything more that you'd like to add to the official debriefing? Anything you might've forgotten at the time?"

Something in my gut said to not say anything about the bell in my pocket. Briar was wanting me to trust him, but the thing of light had asked me to *protect her*. How a bell could be a her, I had no idea, but I was going to do what I could to do that. I wasn't really sure if the bell or the thing of light had saved me, but I owed one or both of them my life.

"Not that I recall. I'm good at remembering details, it's part of ranger training."

"And you always scored well in your training." Agent Briar frowned. "Now, the biggest question is what are we going to do with you? You don't have a pack. Traditionally a new wolf is chosen and turned as part of a ritual. Part of our agreement with the government is that we stick to either breeding the old fashion way, or only replacing wolves who've been killed and then only from people who've been prepared for the change."

"Werewolves can have pups, who knew?" I resisted the chuckle that wanted to well out of me.

"Most people who know about us." Briar drummed on the desk. "But that doesn't help you right now. I think I have an option for you. If it works out, it would be perfect. You'll have easy access to a couple of different VA offices, and there's a fort not far away. How do you feel about returning to the mountains?"

"Mountains?" I'd grown up on a ranch in Montana. My older brother was still running it for my mother after my father had been killed in a freak accident with a mad buffalo.

"Not Montana. The pack there is too large as it is, and too far spread for the Alpha to keep tabs on a newly turned wolf." He kept drumming on the desk. "We've got space in Colorado. The Denver pack recently lost some members to an attempted takeover pissing off the local vampires. There's lots of areas around there where you could settle. You were always good at school. Maybe go to college and figure out a path for yourself."

I held up my hand. "Wait a minute, there's vampires too?"

"And mages, and ghosts, there're a whole lot of things in a paranormal world that you'll come across given time." He turned a thick folder of discharge papers around, slid them towards me, and gave me a pen. "Sergeant Lucas, there's a lot you can do with your life from here on out. It's all up to you."

Leaning forward, I scanned the papers. I tapped the discharge code. "Why PTSD?"

"Trust me, if it doesn't come true after everything you've been through, I'll be surprised."

I didn't know much about werewolves, let alone being one, but the idea of a werewolf with PTSD was a scary one. I hoped he was wrong, but I did understand that more than a few guys, regular guys, ended up showing signs of post-traumatic stress once they got back on the streets and tried to live everyday lives only to have that ripped away from them due to what they'd endured in the service.

"I'll get with the Denver Alpha and have him work with you to find somewhere to live." Briar kept talking as I scanned the rest of the forms. "You've got about a week before we'll know if you survive your first change. That's the most dangerous one."

Looking up from the paper, I stared at him. "There's a chance I won't survive?"

"A lot depends on your wolf. It's a spiritual thing, magical. But if you and your wolf don't bond properly, and you can't endure the pain and disorientation of that first change, you'll die."

If I was going to die, it might be nice to be back in the States. Mom and Lyle might like to be able to bury me in the family plots in the back part of the ranch. For the next hour, I signed the forms ending my military life, one I'd known for nearly fifteen years.

"Let's hope I don't die." I slid the forms across the desk to Agent Briar.

A soft smile spread across his dark face. "I hope not. Now, go clear out your bunk. I want to be in the air in three hours."

"I can be ready in two." I didn't have much beyond my uniforms, my laptop, and a few books.

"Then find me at the airfield. I'll handle talking to your commanding officer and finalizing your discharge." He picked up the papers, tore off the back form, and handed it to me. "Mr. Lucas, welcome to the free world. Hope you survive."

I held the paper, feeling locked in by a strange shadowy world that hadn't been there when I had arrived in Kabul two years earlier. It was amazing how much a couple of years could change someone.

The plane lurched again. The ride after leaving Singapore hadn't been the smoothest. According to the pilot, the weather was supposed to be rough all the way across the Pacific Ocean. Monsoon season was starting early, and there were several storms. It was so bad he said we'd be stopping on Johnson Island instead of going through to Hawaii for refueling. Agent Briar had been fairly set on not caring as long as we got to Colorado as quickly as possible. It was the reason he gave for not taking the safer route that would've taken us through Saudi Arabia and Europe. He hadn't been happy about our nearly twenty-four-hour layover, even if he'd managed to get us one of the nicest hotel rooms I'd ever been in. Of course, he hadn't let me out of his sight the whole time, other than to go to the bathroom. He was treating me like a bomb about to go off, but then if his tale about how my first change might go was true, that might not be far off.

When the plane made a harsh dip then leveled back out, Briar undid his seatbelt and ran for the small restroom in the back of the plane. The big airship was designed to carry entire platoons of soldiers. It felt odd, empty, with just the two of us, some crates, and a dozen or so hummers in the space.

Briar stumbled back to his seat. His dark skin was more than a little green as he fastened his seatbelt back. Through most of the flight, he'd been careful not to look out the windows. I'd flown with guys like him before.

"Deep breaths normally help." I offered.

He nodded. "I know." Then he shook his head. "I'm normally doped up for flights like this, but things aren't great for our kind in Singapore right now and I couldn't find what I needed."

I cocked my head. "They have werewolf Dramamine?"

Briar glanced past me, probably to make sure the cockpit door was closed. Both times we boarded, as soon as we got airborne, he'd taken time to check for any kind of listening devices. The man was hardcore about making sure our secret didn't get out. "Yes. You'll find that most of the normal pharmaceuticals don't work on you anymore. Once you decide on exactly where you're going to settle, we'll put you in touch with a local witch or shaman who can brew up what you need. The alpha I know in Denver has a network of people around him for things like that, well, for almost anything you need."

"That makes it sound like this supernatural world is a lot more complex than I ever thought." Honestly, before my unit had been attacked by the pack of werewolves, I'd never given the supernatural much thought at all. My world hadn't had room for things like strange shadows that could kill people, or shapeshifting men who couldn't be easily killed by a machinegun bullet, or twelve.

"It is. Honestly, there're a lot of people out there who want to do away with the secrecy and just have everyone walk openly in the sunlight."

"Can vampires do that?"

"No." Briar shook his head. "I guess there would still be some of our people who wouldn't be able to be out in the sun. Not just vampires, but if you're lucky you won't ever encounter, or knowingly encounter, some of the worse things out there."

Surprised, I jerked back a little. "There's worse things than vampires?"

Briar sighed. He did that a lot when I asked questions that he thought I either shouldn't be asking or things he figured I already knew about. "Many things. Luckily a majority of them exist on other planes of existence and don't have much to do with ours unless some magic-user is stupid enough to invite them over."

"Demons and such?" It was the only thing I could think of. "Or were the shadows and light things I faced in the chamber from another dimension?"

"I think you may have faced some kind of djinn or deva, maybe both. Since two of them were shadows and one was light, that says different species. Without one to question, it's hard to say. The folks I've got working on it have come up with a few options, but nothing solid. They've found multiple factions in the fire and spirits that were once worshiped in the Middle East. It's possible you dealt with one of them. If, for any reason, you see them again, you call me immediately and I'll dispatch a team."

I wasn't used to being the one calling people for help. Over the years I'd normally been part of the resolution. "I'll do that."

Briar frowned. "If you're prone to lying, you're going to have to get better at it than that."

"What do you mean?" I hadn't been lying, exactly, but he wasn't going to be the first one I called if I ran into more shadows. They needed to pay me back for the loss of the rest of my unit. Briar could have my scraps when I was done with them.

"Don't bullshit me." Briar flashed just a bit of teeth and something deep inside me recoiled, worried about upsetting him. "I've dealt with the military long enough that I know you're thinking they owe you a pound or three of flesh and you're willing to take it. Don't be stupid. It's written on your face. So, if you see a shadow moving funny, you make the call and I'll get people out to you, folks who are more used to dealing with weird things than you are. I may not be required to have you give me an oath, but if you do anything stupid and draw attention to yourself or things around you, I'll come down on you so hard, your grandkids will have chromosome damage. Don't make more work for me and my team. Your alpha won't like it either."

Someone else he hadn't told me much about. Briar was good at telling me all about things while keeping his cards pretty close to his chest. "Okay. If I see anything weird, I'll call. But I want to know what's going on. Don't keep me in the dark."

"I'll do what I can on that front."

"Thank you." I rubbed my hands down my legs. The now-familiar feel of the bell in my pocket was a little comforting. I still hadn't figured out what the being of light had meant when he said to protect her when he gave me the thing.

"What is that?" Briar pointed toward my leg.

"A small bell one of the guys gave to me." I put my hand in my pocket and pulled it out.

Briar sniffed and frowned. "It's silver."

A realization hit me as the small lights above our seats glistened off some of the small etchings on the bell. "Yeah, it is. Should it be burning me?"

"Yes." Briar leaned toward me, eyeing the bell. "Even in your pocket, it should be causing itching. Silver is deadly to us. Some people call it the moon metal. I've never met a shifter who wasn't allergic to it."

Although I'd seen the test results in the file Briar had on me, and felt the strange stirrings deep inside, I couldn't help but ask. "Is there a chance I didn't get infected?"

"No." Briar shook his head. "Everything I've got says you're a werewolf. I can smell the fur under your skin just waiting to come out." He reached tentatively for the bell. "May I?"

Something deep inside me didn't want him to, but couldn't think of a reason to stop him from getting a better look at the bell. "Do we have any kind of antidote for silver poisoning onboard? You know, just in case."

Briar nodded. "I always carry some in my bags. A small blue pouch with silver Celtic knots. Thread, not metal." He did something, and suddenly his fingernails were longer. They weren't claws, but flatter and still somewhat clear like fingernails. He picked up the bell by the small hoop on the top. He moved slowly like he was afraid it was going to swing slightly and brush his fingers.

He held it up and leaned closer. His eyes widened. "I've never seen this language before. It looks like some kind of Sanskrit, but I can't make it out. Do you mind if I get some pictures and send them to my team? It's almost like it's magic. The silver should be burning even my nails and there's nothing." He looked past the bell and focused on me. "You're an odd man, David Lucas. Weird things are happening around you."

I shrugged. "You don't have to tell me."

"Here, you hold it, and I'll photograph with my phone." He passed the bell back to me.

Not being worried about it burning me, I held it up between us.

Briar tapped something on the phone, then frowned. "It's going to need the flash; that might obscure the writing."

"Maybe you can adjust the picture after you take it, or after your team gets it." I looked at the writing. It did look a bit like some of the scrolling script that was all over the buildings in Kabul, but it was different, not exactly like what I'd grown accustomed to seeing.

"That only really works in Hollywood." He tapped his phone.

The flash was bright enough to make me blink.

A shimmer started in the bell. It rocked back and forth in my grasp and a faint purple smoke spilled out of it.

"What are you doing?" Briar looked up from his phone to me.

"No clue." I stared at the bell, worried to drop it, but it wasn't getting hot and I didn't want to hurt it.

"Hold on." Briar tapped his phone again. "I want this on video. I've never seen anything like it."

Chills ran up my arm. I didn't like the weird that was pounding its way into my life. Slamming my free hand over my mouth to keep from inadvertently inhaling the smoke, I looked around for something to put the bell into.

"What in the hell?" Briar stared at the smoke, drawing my attention back to it and the bell.

The purple smoke swirled on the floor, then built upon itself, slowly congealing into something. While the bell stopped smoking, the solidifying mass that stood in the space between my seat and Briar's was the size of a short human.

The bell was lighter than it had been since I'd first held it.

Then a sigh escaped as the smoke cleared leaving a girl in a flowing robe standing there.

"Hold still." Briar yanked his pistol out of his shoulder holster. "Don't move."

She turned toward him and cocked her head, like she was trying to understand him. Then she directed her soft violet gaze toward me. When she smiled, the feeling that kept me holding the bell intensified. The being of light had said protect her.

"Hold on, dude, it's just a little girl." Not letting go of the bell, I moved my hand from my mouth and held it between them.

Briar cocked an eyebrow at me. "You're new to all of this, so I'm going to let a couple of things pass, but just because it looks like a little girl doesn't mean it's not dangerous. And never, ever try to stop an alpha from doing something, unless you achieve alpha status. It's a great way to end up torn to shreds."

I set the bell in my lap and held up both hands, in a universal surrender gesture. I didn't want to cause problems while we were flying above stormy seas. "Sorry. I'm going to have a bit of a learning curve here."

The little girl looked between us, then focused back on me, staring at the bell. A tingle ran through me, lifting every hair on my body.

I shivered.

"No magic." Briar growled as he cocked his pistol.

"Magic." The girl's first word sounded foreign and strange, like her mouth wasn't used to making sounds. It wasn't an accent that I could instantly place. "You don't want magic?"

Briar glared at her. "No, I don't want any magic. What are you? How did you get here?"

She pointed at the silver bell laying in my lap. "David brought me here. Do you have any wishes, David?"

I stared at her. With each word, her strange accent faded and her words sounded more and more like an American child. "How do you know my name?"

"You hold my bell. Until another claims me over your cooling body, we are connected." She straightened her head and ran her hand back over pointed ears, through long red hair that gave off sparks at the motion.

Briar relaxed slightly but kept the gun pointed at her. "Wishes. Claims you. Are you a djinn?"

"Djinn, yes." She frowned. "We are not in the desert. We somehow fly over the ocean. Do you have your own magic?"

"We have a lot of magic, but that's not how we're flying." Briar glanced at me. "Lucas, be very very careful with everything you say while we sort this out."

I wasn't totally dumb to certain things. When I was younger, I watched enough TV to know what a djinn was and how a genie's wish magic could be turned against the wisher. "Got it." I wished he'd put the gun away. I didn't feel that the girl, djinn, meant us any harm, although I didn't like the cooling body she mentioned. I didn't recall any bodies in the hole Carson and I had fallen into. "Do you have a name?"

"I have been called many things over the years by many different men who have owned my bell." For the first time since she materialized from the smoke, she frowned. "I have never been asked to choose a name before."

"Sergeant, be careful with this line of questioning. Names have power." Briar looked like there was a lot more he wanted to say, but he kept his gun and phone pointed at the girl.

The girl nodded. "The grumpy wolf is right. Names define people and things. That is one of the first rules of magic."

"What did your parents call you?" I asked before either of them could say anything else.

"That was a long time ago." She was quiet for a minute.

I looked at Briar who finally put his gun away, but kept the phone out, recording everything that was happening. He just waved at me to keep talking to her, asking her questions. I figured the more intel we gathered, the better.

"When I first left Pashto, my bell was found by a merchant who traveled the Silk Road to Rhome."

"Whoa. Pashto? Where is that?" I'd never heard of the place, but I remember something about Marco Polo on the Silk Road between Rome and China, or something like that.

"It is in the desert south of the great mountains to the east and the ocean to the south." She frowned again.

"Hold on, we need a translator." Briar held out his hand. "Lucas, I don't want to lose any of this, it's incredible. Most people outside of the Middle East have never encountered a djinn before. Give me your phone. Maybe I can get someone to figure this out."

The little girl frowned harder. "Never encountered a djinn before. We are as common as a sandstorm in the desert. How is it possible you do not know of us?"

"Okay, let's take a step back." A thought hit me. "You look like you're about eight. How old are you?

You sound older."

A thoughtful line crossed her face. "We only age when we are outside our vessel, so your counting of time means little to us."

"Do you know how long you were in your vessel this time?" If I couldn't get the information one way, maybe I could come at it from a different angle.

She shook her head and little sparks fell toward the metal floor, dying away before they hit. "Many monsoons have passed since my bell was lost most recently. That does not help, does it?"

"Yes, Agent May, I need some information." Briar rolled his eyes. "Yes, I know this is an unsecured line. It'll be fine. Trust me when you see the video, I'm recording on my phone right now, you'll understand. Right. I'm putting you on speaker." He glanced at me. "Very soon, you won't need speaker to hear people like this, but I'm being nice. Agent May, you're on with David Lucas and a young djinn."

"A what?" The woman's voice rose several octaves.

"A djinn. She was trapped in a bell, falconry bell, I think."

I glanced at the bell, it was small enough to be attached to a bird's leg. I'd seen some in the markets around Kabul and some of the villages my unit patrolled. When Briar named it, it made sense.

"Hold on. Let me pull up the database." In the distance, the sound of a keyboard clacked away. "Right. There is reference to other djinns being trapped in bells, but bottles and lamps are more common."

"So, can you tell me where Pashto is?" Briar asked.

"Give me a second." The keys clacked. "Wow, that one's in Wikipedia."

"So, it's not a different dimension?" Briar looked like his hand holding his phone was getting tired. He extended one finger at a time to stretch them.

"I didn't say that, but we have a record of Pashto being an ancient name for Afghan, so it would make sense it was at least part of modern-day Afghanistan."

The girl walked over and stared at my phone in Briar's hand. "You have a djinn trapped in that small box."

"No." I shook my head. "She's not trapped in the box, she's on another continent. It's a different kind of magic."

"Magic." She nodded. "Yes, that can let you speak long distances. Many of those who held my bell had me send messages back to their families."

"What is she speaking?" Agent May sounded confused. "It sounds like some Afghan dialect, but not one I've heard before."

Agent Briar looked from the phone to the girl. "We're hearing English, but there was some kind of magic right before she spoke."

Magic. Had that been what the tingling had been, the djinn girl trying to figure out how to communicate with us? It would explain the improving, now accent-less English.

"I need everything you've got on her," Agent May requested. "I'll get the team working on this. Are you going to bring her to Washington?"

Conflicting things dashed across Briar's face. "I don't know yet. I'll let you know when I get that worked out."

"I am David's to command." The girl stamped her foot. "None may break that bond, unless you intend to kill him."

Holding up my hands again, I still didn't like the sound of that at all. "Hey, nobody's killing anyone here."

"I have no intention of killing you, Lucas," Briar assured me. "Agent May, get me everything you can on the djinn. We're still a few hours from crossing over into American airspace, if these storms don't send us into the Pacific before that. Meet us in Fort Carson with the data you have."

"I can do that. Maybe I can find a translator spell so I can at least understand her." There was an eagerness in Agent May's voice. "I can only imagine the amount of magical knowledge she holds."

Briar didn't look so sure. "She appears to be about eight or nine, I wouldn't count on her being any kind of massive tome of knowledge."

"We might be surprised." May didn't sound discouraged.

"I'll send you a video as soon as I can. Briar out." He tapped my phone with military efficiency.

Taking the phone back, I looked at the girl standing there with a confused look, like she was trying to take everything in, but not all of it was making sense. When it came to the idea of magic, I knew how she felt.

"Let's go back to a name." I circled the conversation back to something I could follow more easily. "If you don't remember the name your mother or father gave you, was there something others have called you that you liked?"

She grinned. "Several of the men who held the bell before you called me Vash. It is short for Chuvash, the goddess of fire." She beamed a little and her violet eyes lit up.

"Then Vash it is." I grinned. "Now, let's hope you don't burn down too many things."

"If there are things you wish me to burn down, fire is an easy magic to make." Her happy expression darkened for a moment. "It is not always easy to control."

"For now, let's keep the magic to a minimum." Agent Briar rubbed his chin. "How is it you go in and out of the bell?"

"If the bell is in a dark place, it holds me tight until a light releases me." Vash hugged herself and shivered. "I can also be commanded in and out of the bell by the one who holds it." She looked at me so sadly, with down-turned eyes and a slight frown, that something deep inside me cracked. "Please, let me stay out in the light. I was lost in the dark for so long."

Even if I knew the right magic words to return her to the bell, I wasn't sure in that instant I could send her back into the silver.

4

A haze hung between the airstrip and the mountains as Vash and I followed Agent Briar off the C-12 transport plane that had just landed at a special airstrip at the Colorado Springs Airport. Even after we'd cleared the Pacific Ocean, the storms had continued, only clearing when we passed over the Continental Divide, like the high mountains had been what we needed for the last few minutes of clear air. The haze gave the late-afternoon sun a touch of red and orange, but seemed to make the light a little harsher.

Vash glanced everywhere, trying to take in everything at once. Sparks cascaded around her as her hair swayed with each turn of her head. She stopped partway down the stairs and looked back at the huge jet where soldiers were already working on lowering the back hatch to remove the vehicles we'd ridden over with. "That great ship was flying. You have strong magic to make that happen so easily."

Shifting my duffle bag on my shoulder, and biting back a chuckle, I shook my head. "It's science, not magic, that makes planes fly."

"A plane. That is what it is." Vash's face went blank for a moment. "I learned your language from you, Lucas, but there are things I do not understand. Things like this plane."

"And I totally get that." I patted her shoulder. "You've been trapped in your bell for a long time. The world has changed. We…" I glanced at Briar standing there shielding his eyes looking across the tarmac. "I will do what I can to help you get through."

"Thank you, Lucas. I'm not used to the holder of the bell thinking about me, just what I could do for them." Vash smiled up at me.

Something in that soft smile made me want to protect her, not use her. What kind of monsters had the previous holders been that they'd just used her? Over the years, I'd seen enough of the world to understand that not everyone thought the way that I did, or even like the American culture did, but children were supposed to be protected, not exploited. Not since high school had I ever given any thought to being a father, but Vash triggered a parental feeling in me that even my niece and nephew hadn't. I may never know if it was something she was doing to me magically or not, but at that moment, I didn't care.

"There's our next ride." Briar lowered his hand and glanced back at us. "I was starting to think I was going to need to call for a loaner car from the base."

A Jeep roared up to the place, driven by a short woman who looked like she had a lot of Native American blood. Her ruddy complexion was flushed and her long black hair was tied back in a tight braid. She slammed on the brakes bringing the Jeep to a stop so the side door was facing Briar, waiting for him to open it. "You called for a car?"

"Agent May, I didn't know you could drive a Jeep like that—" Briar grinned slightly "—I'm impressed."

"Thank you, Sir. Your flight was a few minutes earlier than I anticipated. You also owe me for dealing with the military who didn't think you qualify for special pickup." She frowned and looked back toward the clouds pushing the haze off the mountains. "There's something interfering with my normally clear vision of things."

I had no clue what she was talking about. Why would clouds interfere with her vision?

Vash nodded as she stared at the Jeep. "The storms are angry. Anger can cloud all vision."

"What do you mean, the storms are angry?" I knelt slightly to be closer to her level. My duffle bag banged against my hip. "Storms are just storms."

"No." Vash shook her head. "Storms have spirits, just like people. You just cannot feel them as such. I am closer to spirit than flesh, most of the time. I feel them. They are very upset. I could ask them why, if you like."

I glanced up at Briar, whose face was unreadable.

"We don't have time for that. We need to get settled for the night. May, after we reach Fort Carson, I also need you to go out and get some clothes for Vash." Briar cast a final glance at the clouds swarming over the mountains.

"Ah, Sir, you do realize I don't have any experience with kids." Agent May looked at Vash and shook her head.

Briar settled into the front passenger seat. "Lucas

and I need to see about getting him transportation and settled in." He held up a finger. "I might have an idea." He pulled out his phone.

I dropped my duffle bag in the back of the Jeep. "Vash, we're going to ride in the Jeep. Is it okay if I pick you up and put you in the seat?" I felt odd asking the little djinn permission for that, but when I stopped and thought about it, it made sense to not just take things for granted. There might be something she wasn't comfortable with and although we hadn't seen a big display of magic, other than her learning English from my mind, I didn't want to inadvertently trigger something that might get explosive. I'd decided to handle her much like live ordnance until I knew better.

"This cart without draft animals to pull it." She touched the Jeep and jerked back. "It's cold iron."

Getting back out of the Jeep, Briar stopped and stared at Vash. "I've got someone on the way to help with the shopping, and other things too. I didn't realize djinn had iron allergies, like some fae. The plane didn't bother you."

Vash glanced back at the plane as the first Hummer rumbled down the rear ramp. "I could feel it around me, but it wasn't against my skin. I never touched it." She took a deep breath and let it out slowly. The sparks in her hair danced around her for a moment. "Maybe this will protect me from the iron."

"If you get uncomfortable, let me know." I picked her up and swung her up into the back passenger seat. She weighed almost nothing. It made me wonder if she was little more than smoke given form, or if it was just because she was so small.

"Thank you, Lucas." She'd stopped calling me David when Briar had kept calling me Lucas. If she was going to be around for a while, I might need to tell her to go back to calling me David. My only friends for years had been my unit, and like everyone else in the military, they used my last name. Only my family called me David.

As I headed around the Jeep to get in, I stopped and stared at the big plane we'd gotten off of. For years, I spent more than my share of time in huge troop carriers flying to different parts of the world. My final flight was over and I wasn't sure how I felt about it. Sure, there weren't going to be people shooting at me, and I wouldn't be shooting back, but was I cut out for civilian life? Somehow it didn't seem fair that the supernatural weren't allowed in the military, or even civilian law enforcement. I understood, but it still didn't seem fair. Werewolves and witches could do a lot to help stop the bad guys that just seemed to be popping up everywhere.

"Are you getting in, Lucas, or are you wanting to jog across town?" Briar grumbled, jerking my attention away from the plane that was just another symbol of the life I was leaving behind.

"Sorry." I jumped in next to Vash and quickly showed her how to fasten her seatbelt before Agent May took off at full speed toward the gate that separated the airstrip from the rest of the airport.

Vash grinned as we slowed. "This is like flying across the ground without using magic." She leaned a little as if trying to keep from touching the side of the Jeep. "This much cold iron would never fly."

May laughed. "You might be surprised. But you're right, these things disrupt a lot of magic. Sergeant Lucas, I guess we'll have to get you something without so much metal in it."

"Probably." I wanted to correct her and remind her I was a civilian now, but couldn't bring myself to say the words. Deep down, I didn't want to be a civilian. I wasn't sure what kind of car I should be looking for either. There were going to be a lot of factors to take in.

Once she cleared the gate and headed across town, May kept her speed to the posted limit, but as the storms began rumbling, the winds kicked up dust and dirt, giving us a sensation similar to her speeding.

It had been years since I had passed through Fort Carson, then I'd been on the way to the Middle East on an early deployment, and we'd been stopping there to finish loading the other unit who was sharing our ride. The trip then had been delayed, like so many things in the military were, by red tape. With a day off duty, I and a few guys from my unit had done a little looking around. The base seemed to have grown in the passing years, but most things were still in the basic utilitarian shapes and colors the military was famous for. Fort Carson had pine trees, not palms. It was up against the foothills, not out in the desert, or less than a mile from the ocean.

Agent May pulled up to a three-story, cinder-block building with a large parking lot. "Okay. Here's your temp housing. We've got two weeks to find you somewhere to live."

The timetable hit me hard. "Two weeks? How am I supposed to find a place in that time? With everything else going on, I'll be lucky to—"

Agent Briar held up his hand. "Sergeant. Don't worry. We've got people who can help you at least find a rental. Tomorrow we'll go up to Denver and start working out where to best look for something."

I huffed. Although I knew he was probably right, it still made me worry. It was a new assignment, and I liked assignments where all the intel was laid out in front of me so I could make informed decisions. Two weeks wasn't going to give me time to get all the info on anything. I didn't even mention that we were going to need some kind of cover ID for Vash.

The young djinn looked around. "It's a stone building, but it's so tall. Like a king's palace. Do many people live here?"

"Yes." Briar stepped out of the Jeep. "Lots of people. Now let's go find your quarters. I requested two bedrooms, since I wasn't sure if you'd be staying in your bell, or not."

As I came around the Jeep to get Vash, she held out her arms to me. "That's up to Lucas. It's nice being out of my bell. I was in there so long."

Agent May glanced around, then let out a sigh that I recognized as an all-clear sound. She must've been worried about someone overhearing us. "If what the person in housing told me is correct, the room is up this way."

Snagging my bag out of the back, I followed Vash who was just a couple of steps behind Briar.

She glanced back at me. "I could make that float for you. Make it lighter."

When she lifted her hand, a tingle ran across my skin and the duffle did get lighter.

"No, Vash." I shook my head. "I don't need you to do that, and I don't think Agents Briar and May will like it if you use magic in public."

"Really?" She pouted slightly, looking even younger than normal. "But does not everyone know of magic?"

"Not everyone." May held the door open for us. "In fact, most humans don't know about magic anymore. You must be careful." She tentatively touched Vash's hair. "And we're going to have to do something about your hair."

Agent Briar nodded. "Yes, we are. I was hoping you might have some ideas about that, Agent May."

May frowned as we all cleared the door and she led us toward the elevator that was just a few feet away. "Because I'm a woman? Look, I realize that a lot of werewolves are stuck in the guise of sexist pigs, but I didn't think you were one of them. But at least you're not thinking of taking them both into protective custody. We aren't equipped for that."

The elevator showed up and we piled in. So far, we hadn't seen another person in the area.

"And Sergeant Lucas is a good enough soldier we don't need to worry about it." Briar looked at me. "He's a top-ranked guy and we can rely on him. If he'd been a civilian, we'd have to work out some other precautions. Vash can't fall into enemy hands. I think he understands that."

"I do." It wasn't something I felt needed to be elaborated on. Vash was triggering protective feelings in me. Someone would have to kill me to hurt her, and from what she'd said on the trip over, that was also the only way they could get her bell away from me.

A knock came from the door while Vash was still in the bathroom playing with the water in the sink. I think she was happy she wouldn't be hauling water into our quarters. It was a feeling I shared. Over the years, I'd been in a few primitive camps where we'd had to lug five-gallon jugs of water in.

Agent Briar went to the door, sniffing before he looked through the peephole. "Ah, they got here fast." He swung open the door.

A man with dark hair and beard stood there. He was shorter than either Briar or me, but had broad shoulders and a bright smile. Beside him was a red-haired woman who didn't look quite so cheerful.

"You got lucky, Agent Briar, we were in the neighborhood." The woman walked in like she owned the place. Her gaze passed over me and landed on Agent May.

The man's smile never faded. "You were a bit vague on the phone, Briar." He kept his eyes lower than Briar's face, and despite his broad shoulders and general powerful look, he was acting submissive to the FBI agent.

"Figured it would be easier to explain it to the two of you when you arrived." Briar glanced out into the hall before closing the door. "You don't have your daughter with you?"

The red-haired woman frowned slightly. "Briar, you might need to update your files, both of the girls are in college now. It kinda frees up some time for us."

Briar locked the door and nodded. "Sorry, things have been busy of late and time gets away from me."

"Their files were updated when they moved out of Cottonwood." May turned slightly from where she'd been working at her laptop. "Briar doesn't keep track of every paranormal in the country. He just doesn't have time."

"Time isn't everything it seems." Vash came out of the bathroom, wiping her hands on a large white towel. "Does everyone have running water now? It must save a lot of time, and stress, particularly for women."

I couldn't help but smile. She was an odd combination of mature and naïve. "Yes, Vash. Well, most do, particularly here in North America. There are still parts of the world where conditions aren't as good."

With wide eyes, the red-haired woman stared at Vash. "What are you?"

Vash turned toward her and stared back. "You're a witch. I believe that's the right word. You're like Agent May." She glanced at the man. "And your man is a werewolf. Are there many werewolves in the world now?"

"No, Vash," Agent Briar spoke quickly. "It just looks that way to you." He pointed to the woman. "I'd like you and Sergeant Lucas to meet Cinnamon and Chad Kilkari. They're part of the local supernatural community."

"Most people call me Cin," Mrs. Kilkari said softly. "And I wouldn't say we're exactly part of the 'local'—" she air-quoted "—community, we're a couple hours away."

Agent Briar nodded slightly. "Right, but you got here quickly. You're also the only members of the community that I could think of quickly who have daughters. Vash here was a bit of a surprise, and Sergeant Lucas doesn't have any children and we'd like some help getting her some clothes and doing something with her hair."

Cin pursed her lips and nodded thoughtfully. "I can see that. The ladies of the Denver pack don't have any little ones. I suppose some of the local witches do, but I'd be happy to help." She squatted down in front of Vash. "Thing is, I still don't know what you are."

Vash glanced to me before answering.

It felt strange to have her silently asking permission. Did she already know about keeping herself secret? Briar and I had mentioned it to her on the plane, but I hadn't honestly expected her to remember it quickly. I nodded. "It's okay."

"I am a djinn. Lucas holds my bell and I am bound to him until he dies." Her voice was a little softer than it had been when she came out of the bathroom, like she was nervous about talking to Cin.

"A djinn?" Cin's eyes widened. "Can't say as I've ever run into one of your kind."

"They tend to be a Middle East supernatural, but even then, there aren't a lot of them around," Agent May spoke quickly. "We have very little information on them."

I cleared my throat. "It's not nice to talk about people like they aren't standing in the middle of the room." It was one of my pet peeves. I liked people to get treated with a certain level of respect.

Agent May paused and stared at me, like I wasn't supposed to interrupt her.

"Anyway" Briar stepped between them. "Cin, if you and Agent May could take Vash to get something suitable to wear. We need her to blend in with the other kids her age."

"May I?' Cin waved for permission to touch Vash's hair.

Again, Vash looked at me. I nodded permission.

"It's okay." Vash looked a little tense.

"Thank you." Cin lifted a lock and a small handful of sparks danced around her hand before falling toward the floor and going out inches from the carpet. "It's incredible. I wish we weren't going to have to find a way to cover it up. Do you know how to control the sparks? The unique color shouldn't be too hard to pass off, but the sparks."

"I was wondering about coloring or some kind of gel," Agent May suggested.

Cin pursed her lips and leaned back as if to better study Vash. "Gel? Maybe. What do we have to work with?" She glanced over her shoulder to Agent Briar.

"What do you mean?" He looked confused.

"Cash, Briar, or FBI card, or something we can

charge. Or would you rather I bill you for what I charge on my cards?" She straightened and stared him down. Maybe it came from her husband being a werewolf, but I was a little surprised at the size of her balls.

Briar nodded. "Agent May, go with Cin and Vash, use your company card. Just keep receipts."

Agent May frowned as she stood. "I don't know anything about kids, and even my civvies are black. Not huge on fashion."

"Not surprised," Cin said. "Sergeant Lucas, do you mind if we go shopping without you?"

I shook my head, then pulled out my wallet. "Take my card. I guess if I'm going to be taking care of her, I might as well start paying for her stuff. And I'm retired now, it's just Lucas, or if you ever get to know me really well, David."

Cin took the card. "Thanks, Lucas. I'll bring back receipts. Until we figure something out, I'll see about casting a glamor on Vash's hair. The girls and I got good with hair glamors."

"That they only use during costume times," Kilkari threw in, speaking for the first time. "Do you need me to drive?"

"Nah." Cin took Vash's hand. "We'll be fine. It's been a little while since I had a little one to shop for. This is going to be fun. You guys stay here and talk werewolf stuff." She looked at me, as if seeing more than just a man standing there. "He's new. Be nice."

Visions of huge bags of expensive clothes filled my mind. I shook my head. "If this helps, keep it fairly simple. I'm a fairly down-to-Earth guy."

Cin looked me up and down. "The camo doesn't help me. Where are you from?"

"Montana." Although Agent Briar trusted the witch, and I was trusting her with Vash, I didn't know how much I wanted her to know about me.

"Plains or mountains?" She opened the door and looked at Agent May.

"Foothills."

"Got it." Cin smiled. "I'll be gentle to your bank account."

"And with Vash." I looked at the young djinn who held her hand like it was a strange unknown sensation, but she was scared to yank free. If Agent Briar hadn't called them, I'd have gone with them, just to make sure everything went fine.

"And Vash." Cin looked down at her and there was a level of genuine warmth in her look. "We'll be fine. This is going to be fun."

"It's okay, Vash." I almost told her she could call me if there was a problem. I'd seen my brother do that with his boys, but she didn't have a phone. Could djinn even use a phone? "You go with Cin and Agent May, have fun and get some new clothes."

She touched her linen robe. "Are my clothes not appropriate?"

"Not for this time, Sweetie." Cin patted Vash's hand. "Come on, we'll be back in a little while. Maybe, when we get done, the guys can meet us for dinner."

"That's a good idea." Agent Briar held out his hand to Agent May. "Keys to the Jeep would be useful for that."

"Okay." As she handed over the keys, May had a pleading look on her rusty features, saying louder than words that she wasn't looking forward to shopping.

For the first time since I had met her, I felt a little sympathy for the witch. Shopping wasn't my favorite thing to do either.

The door closed as they went down the hall, and Agent Briar looked at Kilkari. "Okay, now, I need an update on the Denver pack status. I presume you're still attending full moon with them."

Kilkari claimed the chair Agent May had been in. "Yeah, I've missed a few meetings due to business mostly. Mark understands, as long as I let him know and have a good reason." He rubbed his head for a moment. "Sending me to Mark was a great call, and the moons I've had to spend away from the pack can be hard. At least I'm not having nightmares anymore."

I sat down on the ledge of the window. "Nightmares? This whole thing causes nightmares?" Nightmares were something I was used to. A lot of combat veterans had them. I was lucky and mine hadn't led to PTSD. Some nights I could still hear the howls as the pack tore my unit to shreds, but that was the only nightmare I'd had since the attack.

The two men looked at each other.

"Not normally," Briar said first. "Sometimes things happen, just like with humans, and we get them. Kilkari here ate the sheriff. He was defending Cin and their handyman, but after that, I sent him to the closest alpha, who happens to be Mark in Denver.

You'll meet him tomorrow."

Studying Kilkari, I pointed. "So, you got to eat a sheriff and didn't get jail time? I'm guessing there's different rules for us." Even though Briar had explained a lot of what his new life was going to be, he hadn't said they could kill law enforcement and get off.

"Special case." Kilkari shook his head. "And I really don't advise killing people. It can really mess you up and they taste horrible. But like Briar says, he was threatening Cin and RJ, well, the sheriff and his wife. I didn't eat that much of him, and luckily Briar's team was on site quickly to handle the clean-up. The other thing was, I didn't have an alpha or a pack to help me through the first year." He frowned. "Cin did her best. I have no idea what I would've done if I hadn't had a witch for a wife. I used to be a cop down in Cottonwood. I got attacked in the line of duty, and the local hospital didn't have any antidote. By the time I would've driven to Pueblo, or up here, it would've been too late anyway, so I didn't even bother."

"And I didn't find out about him," Briar took over, "until one of my seers spotted a disturbance in Cottonwood. It still took me several days to track down him and his wife, just as they were dealing with the Sheriff and his wife. Once I figured out what he'd been through, I connected him with the Denver alpha, who has decades of experience in dealing with new strays."

"Strays?" I wasn't sure I liked the sound of the word. "Is that what we are?"

"A lot of packs feel that any wolf who isn't connected to a pack is a stray," Briar said. "We didn't get to that before Vash showed up."

I nodded as a question came up. "What am I going to do with her during the full moon?"

Kilkari shrugged. "Maybe we can get Cin to babysit for you. It's not like you can just get one of the neighborhood kids to come do it for you."

"Or maybe some of the other locals might have some ideas," Briar suggested. "There's not a lot of shifters in Colorado Springs, but there are a couple. There's also a coven here. I trust the leader and he might be a good resource for you."

"How long are you planning on staying?" Kilkari raised an eyebrow.

"Not sure yet." Briar looked at his phone. "Right now, there's nothing major going on, so I have a few days. Vash is special. We haven't had a djinn on American soil in a long time. The ones in the Mid-East stay away from us. There's rumors they have some dealings with the elves, but they avoid the rest of us. We have no idea the extent of their powers. There's too much we don't know, and if Vash can help us learn things, that would be good."

My protective side swelled up a little. "You're not going to pressure her or anything like that." Deep inside me, something growled.

Briar held up his hands and shook his head. "No, we don't operate like humans. I am going to ask you to give us regular reports on her progress and things like that, but I'm not going to torture her or do anything invasive to get the information she might possess. We're going to need to get her comfortable here and see what happens." His phone rang, and Briar frowned. "Give me a moment."

Kilkari and I both nodded as he answered the call.

"So, I've never been around kids, well, not since I was a kid, and I was a boy, not a girl, a magical girl." I realized I'd babbled a bit as I looked at Kilkari.

He chuckled. "And magical girls make all the difference. I bet djinns are a little different from witches. But at least you're getting her early enough to make an impact before the terrible teens hit. When she starts bringing love interests home, growl a lot, and clean guns. If that doesn't drive them off, you've either found a good one or a bad one. Trust your instincts."

I held up a hand and shook my head. "I don't want to think about that right now. Since she came out of the bell, I've been feeling a strange protectiveness that I've never felt before. I can't even start thinking about boys, girls, or whatever at this point. I'm afraid I'd eat them like you did the sheriff."

Kilkari laughed again. "By then you'll have a lot more control and nobody's going to die, I hope."

Briar growled as he slipped his phone in his pocket, then walked over to the window and looked out.

"What's wrong?" Kilkari asked.

"A few hours ago, we had a report from one of our agents on the west coast about a magical disturbance crossing over into continental airspace." Briar left the window and headed for the door. "Now the local coven leader says there's something that just came over the mountains."

"Where are you going?" I jumped off the window ledge and followed him.

"The roof." Briar opened the door and headed out.

I glanced at Kilkari and he was already out of his seat following Briar. There wasn't really a choice. Deep inside me that feeling that Briar said was my wolf, growing while waiting to emerge with the moon, pushed me to follow Briar. If an alpha as powerful as he appeared to be was worried about something, the young wolf shot terror through me. It wasn't a feeling I liked.

A flight of stairs at the end of the hall took us up to the roof. The wind whipped around as we walked toward the edge looking toward the two mountains. There was something in the wind that caused the hair on my arms to rise. It tingled across me, like it was searching for something.

Agent Briar lifted a ring high and closed his eyes.

The tingling ended as suddenly as it started.

"Okay, that was different." Kilkari rubbed his arms and shivered.

Briar pulled out his phone and tapped it a couple of times before putting it to his head. "Really?" He jerked the phone away from his head. "I had signal in the damned building."

Kilkari shrugged. "Colorado. It all depends on where you are. The landscape messes with signal something fierce. Who are you trying to call?"

"May." He glared toward the mountain. "They need to get back here. This storm isn't natural."

As Kilkari had done, I rubbed my arms. The tingling was slowly fading. "And you blocked it with a magic ring?"

Briar sighed. "Not sure if you'll ever learn, but sometimes it's not good to question an alpha."

"Or a general, but I've done that too." I smiled slightly as he tilted his head. I wasn't going to have to worry about generals anymore. Maybe I could get along with alphas better than I had most of the recent pompous asses who'd gotten in charge of the military.

"I think I'm going to like you." Kilkari punched me in the shoulder. "But yeah, he did a magic thing to make their magic not sense us." He pulled his phone out. "Let me get ahold of Cin and tell them to hightail it back. If we're lucky they haven't even reached the closest store."

Briar sighed again and rubbed his hands over his short reddish hair. "The ring has a cloaking spell on it. I can either do just myself, or something a little larger. Don't move too far away, or you'll be outside the spell."

I pointed at him. "Magic. Got it. Lots to learn." Curves, there were always learning curves and I was going to need to stay on top of this new one if I was going to keep Vash safe. I didn't even have any real idea what kind of magic she could do, what limits her power had. There were always limits. Even Briar couldn't help us much there, as he didn't have much information about djinn.

"Cin," Kilkari's voice was raised as he held the phone to his ear. "Can you hear me?" He frowned. "Hon, head back to the base." He pulled the phone away and stared at it, tapping the screen before slipping it back in his pocket. "Lost the signal."

"Let's hope they heard enough." Briar stared up at the clouds. "It's almost like the clouds themselves are alive. There's something in this storm. Something dark and angry."

"Storms can't be alive." I looked up into the rolling darkness above us that spread out from the mountains and cast across the plains to the east. They darkened the landscape, casting long shadows that lashed about like a nest of snakes. Vash has said something about storms having spirits. Could that mean they were alive?

"Depends on the storm," Agent Briar muttered. "We might want to get back inside. My ring protects us from magical eyes, but not casual observation. Something tells me these clouds see on several levels."

Kilkari headed for the door that would take us to the stairs. "And here I thought having a ghostly mother-in-law was the most irritating thing in the world, but clouds that can see, that feels more invasive."

Briar chuckled as he followed Kilkari. "Djinn are elementals. I might not have dealt with a djinn, but I have encountered a couple other forms of elementals over the years. Yes, they have abilities those of us who are of solid don't."

"Solid?" I held the door open as Briar started down the stairs.

"Another term you'll begin to understand. Think of the smoke Vash appeared out of after the light went through her bell." Briar kept his voice just loud enough to carry to Kilkari and me. "We can assume other djinn and their like can be smoke and other elements. We can assume the legends of their power are correct." He glanced back at the door that was nearly shut. "I don't like things I don't totally understand."

That was something I could agree with. "With you on that. Been fighting in the Mid-East and Africa for years. Each area is different, but for the most part, the people are the same. We know how to respond to them. Guess I'm going to have to learn how to respond to different people."

"Exactly." Briar stopped at the first landing and looked back at me, giving me a soft smile. "You might actually take to this new life fairly easily."

"I hope so." All my life I'd dealt with change, but I'd also always known where I was going. I no longer knew that for sure.

Kilkari reached the door onto our hall. "Cin and I will be happy to lend a hand comprehending this new path you're walking. Not saying we understand everything, but we have good contacts and are pretty good about figuring things out as they come flying at us."

It wasn't an exaggeration to say I had no idea how to deal with what was flying at me; all of it was new and different. "I appreciate it. I figure I'll be leaning on you a lot as I get this all sorted out."

A tall, limber man stood outside the door of my apartment. He was dressed in a blue tie-dyed T-shirt that matched the cap over his pale blond hair. Turning slightly, he smiled. "Three werewolves in temporary housing on an army base, maybe y'all might know why there's a swarm of effrit coming across the mountains."

Agent Briar stopped and put his hands on his

hips. "I thought you knew I'm not big on questions, Mr. Harris."

Mr. Harris didn't back down. He was the first man I'd seen who didn't instantly bow to what Briar wanted. "So, you bring a parcel of trouble to *my* town and think I'm going to just sit back and do nothing?"

Briar cocked his head. "Does it help that I didn't mean to bring a pack of effrits to Colorado. You're sure it's an effrit that we're dealing with?"

"What else could it be?" Mr. Harris froze, then frowned. "And a djinn…I think. Where in the hell did you get a djinn?"

My heart raced, and deep inside me, a wolf growled protectively. "How do you know about her?"

The door to my room opened and Cin Kilkari stepped out. "There you guys are. What's going on?" She glanced at Harris. "Gavin? Gavin Harris? What are you doing here?"

"You know him?" Briar pointed at Harris.

Cin nodded as she opened the door wider. "Yes. He's the local high priest. We've crossed paths a few times, and a mutual friend has mentioned him occasionally."

"Ah, Cin, so you're tangled up in this too?" Harris took a step closer to the door.

I stepped in front of him. I didn't know him, the wolf inside me didn't like him, and I wasn't going to let him near Vash, whom I could feel inside the room. They hadn't had time to get back from wherever they'd gone, but I knew she was there. "I think you need to stop."

Briar touched my shoulder, and my wolf

instantly backed down. "It's okay, Lucas, he's one of the good guys. I'd planned on introducing you soon. He kinda runs the local supernatural community."

Harris didn't look like much. I frowned, stopping just shy of snarling at him. He didn't feel strong enough to run the community. With everything I'd been dealing with since the werewolf attack nearly a month earlier, I figured there had to be more to the skinny man than appeared.

"Lucas." Vash ran out of the room. "You are all right. The effrit didn't get you." She stopped a foot or so from me and looked up.

"Yes. Agent Briar had protections." Nodding, I gave her a soft smile. There was no way I could give her anything but. She radiated innocence. The wolf deep inside me smiled too. It liked her. I couldn't tell where its feelings stopped and mine began. Maybe, after I learned more about what it meant to be a werewolf, I would understand where the wolf inside me ended and I began, if there was a true separation.

"Good." She looked Briar over, her gaze lingered on his hand. "But I doubt your trinket will be of much use when the effrit figure out where they need to attack."

Pointing toward the door, I turned Vash that direction. "Let's take this into the room."

"Good idea." Agent Briar waved everyone back in.

Inside the room, Agent May sat on the bed, looking pale under her ruddy complexion.

"What's wrong, May?" Briar stopped a couple of feet from her.

May's hands in her lap shook slightly. "She teleported us back. I've never endured something like that before."

Briar turned slightly and stared at Vash. "Teleported? You can teleport people?"

Vash spread her hands slightly. "Only short distances. As I get older, I can go farther."

"That's good to know." Agent Briar smiled and went to look out the window.

Harris looked at Vash as Kilkari closed the door. "You're young, for a djinn. Can't say as I ever ran into one so young."

"You've run into djinn before?" May looked from Harris to Briar. "There are no records."

"Are you surprised?" Harris crossed his arms. "Agent May, have you recorded everything you know into the agency files?"

Agent May glared at him, but didn't say more.

Her silence was as much an admission as if she'd said, "Yes."

Cin Kilkari spoke first. "I think every family has its own records and knowledge it holds sacred. We also stumble on things in our studies."

Harris smiled and nodded. "Exactly. I did a lot of traveling in my time."

The building shook.

I stared out the window. The skies were darker than before.

"I don't think we're as hidden as I would like," Briar growled.

May jumped up from the bed. "We're going to have to protect ourselves."

"No. There are innocents in this building." Cin Kilkari ran toward the door. "We need to take this outside. If they hit the building to get to us, maybe we can protect people by moving the fight."

"Do you know how to fight an effrit?" I started after her.

"No, but I can throw fireballs with the best of them." Cin jerked the door open.

"Ice and water work the best against effrit." Harris followed her. "They are creatures of fire and smoke."

Vash took my hand. "He is right. I can protect you, but I'm not strong enough to defeat one effrit, let alone six."

Harris spun around and stared at us. "Six? I'm not sure I like those odds."

Briar knelt in front of Vash as another wave of magic struck the building.

Around us, the base alarms began blaring. It would be minutes or less before soldiers swarmed the area. Regular army men and women wouldn't be able to do anything against a magical attack.

"Is there anything you can do to help us, Vash?" Briar stared into her face. "Could you move all of us somewhere else? Somewhere that would protect the innocent people around us?"

"Where?" Vash's voice was softer than it had been. "My energies are low."

"We could augment your energies," Harris offered. "The drawback is if we end up in a battle afterward, we would all be weakened. We're going to need magic to defeat them, or evade them."

"Then evade we should." Cin put her hand on Briar's shoulder. "If we were in Cottonwood, I would have suggestions for safe houses. Here… no."

"Then it's good that you've got someone local here." Harris smiled weakly. "It's not much, but I know of a witch not far from here. Her shields are strong and we can disappear from all magical searching. But I don't like the idea of hiding under the protection of one of my coven."

"Then we won't stay long." Briar stood. "I take it she is somewhere here on the base."

Harris shook his head. "No. But close by. Closer than the shopping center you went to."

Another wave of magic hit the building.

I wasn't used to being uncertain as to what to do. Magic and those creatures that wielded it was new to me. If we'd been faced with insurgents, I'd have known how to take up a rifle and fill them full of lead. I'd have understood to look for them deep underneath buildings and watch them for evidence of roadside bombs. But with magic, I had no idea what to look for, or what I was up against.

"Then let's move out." Briar frowned as plaster rained down on us.

The building was beginning to weaken.

"Can you pull the image of where we need to go from my mind?" Harris knelt next to Briar. "If not, I think I can push it to you."

Vash glanced at me, but didn't wait for my nod before looking back at him. "I can see where you want to go. It is as you said, close by. I can carry three at a time. But I might not be able to move more."

"We'll help," Harris assured her. "I'll go with you on the first one, to make sure we don't surprise Garnet. She isn't used to people just showing up in her house unannounced."

"Take Cin and Chad with you on the first go," Briar instructed as another magical blast shook the building.

More plaster came down on us, and several of the cinder blocks in the outer wall shifted inward.

Cin and Kilkari stepped closer to Vash, as Harris took her hand.

Something tightened in my gut. She was supposed to be mine to protect. This was different from the shopping trip. We were under attack and it might be possible the opponents would feel her using her magic. I didn't know how that all worked, but Harris had felt us in his area, so it stood to reason the effrit would also sense her.

Vash's hair sparked more violently than normal. It turned to smoke first. Tendrils of it wrapped around the others, engulfing them, blocking them from view. As the window across the room exploded, sending shards of glass around us, the smoke faded and they were gone.

Agent May made a series of gestures and Briar raised his ring.

A smoking skeleton that reminded me of the one in the cave where I'd found Vash flew through the window. It howled and lunged at us.

May's magic and Briar's ring created a glowing dome over us.

"Damn, they're ugly." Briar glared and clenched

his fist. The ring on it glowed.

I wanted something to do. Against the effrit, I was helpless. I wanted a magic ring, wand, or shotgun that could even the odds. After years as an army ranger, I wasn't used to that feeling. It sucked.

Two effrit made it through the window and all we could do was stand there in the room with the glowing dome protecting us.

Vash's bell in my pocket grew warm, and her purple smoke poured out of my pocket for several seconds before she materialized in front of me.

She smiled. "It is very close, but the shields are so tight that the effrit will not know we are there." Vash took my hand.

"Good." Briar put a hand on her shoulder, followed by May.

Again, Vash's hair sparked and turned to smoke. A soft warmness filled me as her magic took over. Then the whole world turned grayish purple and the room faded away.

Effrit screams filled my ears and Vash laughed. Her mirth was like a ringing bell. The sound was one of the most comforting things I'd ever heard.

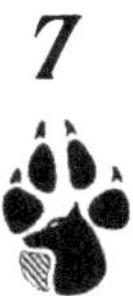

7

The world solidified again. A wall of videos filled my sight. A pungent scent hit my nose. It reminded me of the smell of the market back in Kabul. I wrinkled my nose and shook my head.

"That was different," Briar muttered as he stepped away from Vash.

Vash wobbled, then collapsed. Her body dissolved into smoke before I could grab hold of her. The gray smoke was paler than any of the other times I'd seen it. A tendril of it rushed into my pocket, and the bell there grew warm as every last bit of it disappeared in there.

I grabbed for the smoke, but it was gone too quickly. "What happened? Where is she?" I looked frantically around.

Briar put a hand on my shoulder.

I shook it off. "Do you know? What happened?" I snarled and glared at him.

"Easy there, pup." Harris held his hand up, stepping between us. "She's tired. Moving us here quickly and surely was a bit much for her. She's young. Even young djinn have limits to their powers. When a djinn is tired, they retreat to the item they're bound to." He pointed at my pocket. "I'd say that item is in your pocket."

Just as I started to reach and pull out the bell, I stopped. Even though Briar said Harris was one of the good guys, I wasn't totally sure of that. I wanted to make my own decisions as to who was trustworthy and who wasn't. "So that's why her smoke went into my pocket, I'm her guardian?"

Harris stepped back and relaxed his stance. "Where did you hear that term?"

"A being of light entrusted me with her safety." I put my hand in my pocket. There was a faint difference in the way the bell felt from how it had been when Vash had been standing there near me. It was warmer and slightly heavier.

"I've heard of beings of light." Harris rubbed his short red beard thoughtfully. "Even in all my travels, I haven't encountered one. You should count yourself lucky, luckier still that he entrusted you with Vash. I wonder why the effrit are after you."

There was an empty chair behind us. The Kilkaris were already seated on the overstuffed couch as was an athletic-looking woman with long black hair. She appeared to have Native American blood, but less than Agent May. Like Harris, she wore tie-dye, but a long dress, not a T-shirt.

"Ah, where are my manners? Mr. Lucas, may I introduce Garnet Godfree, my priestess. Garnet, this is Mr…" Harris looked at me. "Sorry, but I didn't get your first name."

"Mr. Lucas is fine." I took a deep breath, forcing my momentary panic back deep inside. I didn't need to let her see any of the feelings that were racing through me. "It's good to meet you, Ms. Godfree."

She smiled. "Welcome to my home, Mr. Lucas. I have to say that I've never had anyone materialize in a plume of smoke before. Magic can be a strange and wonderful thing, can it not?"

Returning her smile, I inclined my head slightly. "I'm still getting used to it. Can't really say that wonderful is a term I'd use just yet, but strange it definitely is."

Godfree laughed. "Many people on their first steps into our world feel that way. Sit, Mr. Lucas. Let Gavin help you understand your new world a little better."

Briar put his hands behind his back and stared at Gavin. "How about before we do that Gavin explains to me how he knows so much about djinns and effrits."

Harris chuckled. "Agent Briar, there's a lot of things the Infragilis Council doesn't know. As much time as we spend hiding from the mundanes, there are parts of the supernatural community that hide from the Infragilis Council. Creatures like the djinn and effrits see them as a creation of the West, and not to be trusted. The biggest question that I've got is why they entrusted a newly turned werewolf, an obvious member of their military, with a young djinn?" He pointed at me, more specifically my leg and the pocket where Vash's bell rested. "No bound djinn has been allowed outside their control in over two hundred years. Why now? Why Vash?"

I sank into the empty chair, my legs suddenly not able to support me. These were questions that I hadn't stopped to ponder, but until that moment, I hadn't had the information to ask them. A fire darkened inside me. Information, how much had Briar just skimmed the surface of because he either felt that I wasn't ready to deal with it, or his superiors didn't feel it was important enough to give to me?

"That being of light who gave her to me, what was it?" I glared at Briar as I gripped the arms of the chair. Deep inside me, the wolf growled until Briar looked at us. Then it went silent.

"I don't know." His words were carefully balanced, level without any inflection.

Turning my attention to Harris, I softened my stance. I might not know him, but to that point, he'd been more forthcoming with information than Briar had. "How about you?"

A soft smile split Harris' red beard. "I like you. Stronger than some who become wolves." He patted Briar on the shoulder. "Lucky you're not going to have to deal with him."

Understanding the undertones, I shook my head. "I have no urge to be in charge of shit. All I want is information so I can keep Vash safe. What was the thing of light? Some kind of angel or something?"

Harris laughed again. "For all the strength of the church, their founders and mythology left this world a long time ago. Angels and demons aren't something we have to deal with in this day and age."

"There're enough other things out there to keep us busy." Cin leaned against Kilkari on the couch. "Gavin, stop dancing around the question. He deserves to know, and I'm curious. Can't say as I've ever run into a being of light, but then Vash is my first djinn too."

"Okay." Harris nodded solemnly. "There's a lot out there that could fit your description. I'm presuming it was fighting the effrits."

"Yes." I didn't take my eyes off him as I dipped my chin in acknowledgment.

"Then it wasn't a partially formed Valkyrie. Since it was in Afghanistan, it wasn't a Native American spirit. It could be something from the Hindu pantheon, but I doubt it." Harris hummed slightly. "I figure it was a higher djinn of some sort or a fey."

"Which brings us back to, why it would give the bell to me?" When I touched my leg, the bell was still warm in my pocket.

"Was it outnumbered? Injured?" Harris didn't seem to react to my accidental mention of the bell.

"Both, although it defeated them before telling me to take care of her." So much had been happening, it was hard to remember the details of everything down in that hole. "Something about her liked me."

Harris pursed his lips and closed his eyes for a moment. "That makes me lean stronger toward a higher djinn, they believe in freedom and free will."

"Freedom? Then why are their kind bound to lamps and such?" That didn't sound like the way a race that believed in freedom would act.

"Legends say there are always reasons why djinn are bound to something," Garnet spoke before Harris could. "Sometimes they are criminals."

"She's a little girl. What kind of criminal could

she be?" That didn't feel right, didn't make sense.

"Their rules are different from ours." Harris scratched his beard. "It might have also been to keep her safe. The thing is, we won't know why she was bound to the bell unless she happens to know. I'm guessing neither one of you thought to ask her."

Briar threw up his hands. "We didn't even discover she was in the bell until we were flying over the Pacific."

"Which still gave you time to ask her." Harris frowned at Briar. "Seriously, you people who think you know everything and are quick to start pushing others around don't know half as much as you think."

"Mr. Harris, if you're about to go all hippy shit on me, you can leave." Briar glared.

Garnet stood and walked up next to Harris, shielding the rest of us from Briar. "Or you can. This is my house, not some super-secret bunker where people never leave once you have them there."

Agent May put a hand on Agent Briar's arm. "Back down. If we go out while the effrits are still in the area, there's a chance they'll feel the djinn's magic on us and come for us. We've got a big enough mess to clean up on base, and they listen to your barking and badge."

With a long exhale, Briar turned. "Okay, you're right. We need a team of telepaths on the ground there to make sure everything's taken care of."

"Get control of yourself and I'll make the call." May patted his arm, then pulled out her phone and headed for the kitchen.

Cin straightened and looked at me. "Sergeant

Lucas, this is something you're going to have to get used to. I can say it's the first time I've seen Agent Briar pushed this far, but all werewolves find their limits have changed from what they used to be. Even if you think you normally have your emotions under control, this is going to be all new to you, and it's not just your emotions that you have to control, but those of your wolf too."

Her words made sense. The wolf inside me kept trying to make its way out, and influence me, even though I didn't want it to. Since I had met Briar, I hadn't seen him lose it. There was something a little reassuring about him not maintaining as much control as he always seemed to have. Over the years, I'd known a lot of guys like him. They were always in control until they were pushed too far, then they cracked. The odds were that Briar wasn't used to people questioning him. Harris had done that. Maybe Briar needed to learn how to deal with more people who didn't always bow to everything he wanted.

Harris took a deep breath and lowered his gaze. "Look, Briar, Sorry for pushing your buttons. It's one of the things I'm good at."

Agent Briar glared at him. "You might learn to rein it in a bit when dealing with shifters, Gavin. I realize that there aren't a ton of them around Colorado Springs, but there are a few, so be careful."

"I know." Harris put his hands in his pockets and shuffled his feet slightly. "Really, sorry. Maybe I've just gotten used to the pack up in Woodland who takes care of the elderly wolves."

I stared at him. "Wait a minute, there's a home

for werewolves around here?" Another thing I'd had no idea about, but somehow assisted living for werewolves, or supernaturals sounded dangerous.

Harris spread his hands. "Well, not just elderly werewolves, but also wolf-weres, wolves who turn human a couple of nights a month. It's complicated. They're good people, but they're also one of the reasons so many supernaturals avoid the area, well, other than a few lone shifters, bigfoots, and human magic users."

"And bigfoot is real." I shook my head. "Sure, why not, all the other monsters are real. Vampires too."

"Oh yeah, we have a couple of non-humans in the Springs." Harris paced in a small circle. "There's a fairly large coven of vampires in Denver. They like more populated areas, easier to find donors that way."

"We didn't get to all details of things on the flight," Agent Briar interrupted. "Vash's arrival threw me off track." His phone rang. He pulled it out, glanced at it, and then frowned. "I need to take this." He headed for the kitchen where Agent May was still making other calls.

"He's always like this." Kilkari turned slightly, watching Briar go. "He'll introduce you to Mark, the alpha in Denver. Mark's cool. Really laid back for an alpha."

Harris nodded slightly. "He is. I like the way Mark runs the pack up there and keeps track of the other wolves around the area."

Briar came back, still frowning. "Agent May and I are going to have to head back to Fort Carson." He looked at Garnet. "Any chance you can give us a lift, since we left the loaner Jeep there?"

Garnet stood slowly. "Sure. Gavin can keep my shields in place if something comes poking around." She glanced at Harris. "You might want to call for some takeout."

Cin rose as well. "If you have room, Chad and I really should head home. Since it looks like finding some clothes for Vash is out right now, we've got a couple of things to take care of."

Kilkari stood next to her. "Yeah, we've got to get things ready for the full moon. I don't like to leave too many things outstanding for Cin to worry about while I'm out of pocket."

Feeling uncomfortable with so many people standing over me, I eased out of the chair. "Speaking of, Agent Briar and I were talking about what I'm going to do with Vash during the moon, or the evenings of the moon, or however that works." I hated sounding like I didn't know something, but the truth was, I was just starting on the learning curve of being a werewolf.

Cin cocked her head and looked at me. "Well, you could either bring her down to me, or I could come up here."

"We could help too," Harris offered. "Hey, Cin, why don't you come up and do full moon with us and we can chat with Vash, try to make her feel more at home."

"Sounds like fun." Cin smiled. "Okay. We'll work out the details over the next couple of days."

May came out of the kitchen. "Got a team of

telepaths on the way. Also, have a cover-up story going out to the media of a microburst hitting to explain the building damage. By tomorrow morning nobody on base will even think about flaming skeletons hitting the building. We're still working on a way to contain the effrits, so Vash is going to need to either stay in her bell or under a shield."

"Next time she comes out, I'll talk to her about it." I wasn't exactly sure how that was going to work, but I'd figure out something.

"Good. We'll be back after we've done what we can tonight." Agent Briar headed toward the door.

I glanced at Harris, wondering if he was going to be a bit more forthcoming with info than Briar had been. It looked like the two of us were going to have some time alone, until either Vash came back out of the bell, or Briar, May, and Garnet returned. I wasn't great at small talk with people I didn't know real well, but with my unit gone, strangers were all I had left in the world.

Glancing around, I did my best to hide the anxiety that built up in me as Garnet led Vash and me into the store. For the third time since we got out of the rental truck, I wiped my hands on my camo pants. I knew both Vash and I needed clothes so we could blend in, but I wasn't sure it was a good idea for us to go into such a crowded place. From what Harris had said, the effrit could change shape. There could be any number of them in the store and I wouldn't know it until they attacked. Sure, Garnet or Vash might sense them, but I didn't like the idea of not being the first one to pick up on potential danger.

"Okay, let's go over here and see what we can find." Garnet navigated through the crowds like an expert shopper. "They're just starting to put out the back-to-school clothes, so there should be plenty of things for us to find for Vash."

"Are all of your markets so busy?" Vash clung to my hand as we trailed after Garnet.

"Not all of them." I wished we'd gone somewhere at one of the close small towns that might have been a little less crowded.

Vash nodded. "I've never been to an indoor market before. When last I was free of my bell, everything was done in outdoor markets."

"Big stores are fairly new to our culture as well." I dodged around a woman who had stopped to pull a box off an endcap. She glanced in our direction with a confused look. Over the years, I'd learned to blend in almost anywhere. We were going to need to watch what we said. I was thankful that between Cin Kilkari and Garnet, they'd managed to get Vash to find a way to hide the sparks that were natural to her hair so she didn't stand out.

"Ssshhh." Garnet put a finger to her lips, subtly telling us that we needed to watch what we were talking about. "Ah, here we go. Little girls' section."

Racks of pastel T-shirts and pants spread over that section of the store. There were a few dresses and skirts scattered among them. Mothers and children were pulling things off the racks and some ended up in buggies and some were returned to the racks.

"Where do we start?" I muttered, trying to figure out what we needed to do. It would've been nice if the effrits had held off their attack on temp base housing until Cin and May had managed to find Vash some clothes.

Garnet frowned. "A buggy. We need a buggy. Lucas, can you run back up front and grab a shopping cart? We'll start looking. Any color that you prefer we avoid?"

Why on earth was she asking me about color for Vash's clothes? I shrugged. "No clue. Just make her look nice."

Vash frowned. "You don't think I look nice?"

I knelt, not wanting to upset her about anything.

"We need us both to blend in a bit more. You don't see any of the other little girls wearing these kinds of robes, do you?" I touched the sleeves of her gray, light-weight robe. "Back in Afghanistan that would've been fine, here, it stands out."

"Oh." Vash smiled. "I understand."

"So, go find a buggy." Garnet waved for me to leave.

It wouldn't take me long to get to the front of the store and grab a cart. Garnet had proven she could hide from the effrit. Vash was safe. I couldn't help myself, I took long strides as I wove through the other shoppers. The faster I got the buggy and returned to them, the sooner the strange feelings of abandoning Vash would fade.

As I touched the buggy, a growl welled up inside me. I turned around, wishing it was possible to see supernaturals around me. Something or someone was nearby. My wolf was growing stronger with each day. We hadn't made it to Denver yet, in preparation for the full moon. I really hoped that meeting with Mark, the Denver alpha, would start me on the path of controlling the wolf inside me. With luck, I'd just inadvertently crossed another shifter's path and my wolf had reacted, leaving me totally clueless.

Tightening my grip on the shopping cart, I hurried to where I'd left Garnet and Vash.

When I met up with them, Garnet was talking to a tall blond man in a tan uniform. He looked military, complete with a crew cut, but I didn't recognize the badge on his shoulder.

Vash was holding up a light green shirt with a

unicorn on it. She turned slightly and smiled. "What do you think, Lucas? I haven't seen a unicorn in a long time. I thought they were gone."

"They are." I stopped the cart and smiled.

"Not exactly." The big blond grinned. "But we don't talk about them much."

Unicorns weren't something I wanted to stop and think about, particularly with a bunch of humans moving around us. "The shirt would go well with your hair." It at least sounded like something I should say. There were things I never expected to do, and trying to tell a little girl what kind of shirt to buy was one of them. Being Vash's guardian was going to be a lot more challenging than anything I'd ever done before. The odds were that there would be little things popping up for a long time. I never wanted a family beyond the one I'd grown up with or my unit. Maybe if I had, I'd have a better understanding of what I was supposed to do with such things as talking about unicorns.

"That's what I told her." Garnet put a couple of other shirts into the cart. "Lucas, I'd like to introduce Brock Summers. He's part of the…ah…local community."

Summers held out his hand and smiled. "Hi. You're what I—" he dropped his voice to the barest of whispers "—smelled—" then returned to a normal volume "—as I walked in. New in town, I take it."

I returned his firm handshake, trying to not squeeze too hard as my wolf growled and the urge to dominate a lesser species surged through me. Whatever Brock was, it wasn't a wolf. "That's right.

Just ah…retired from the Army." The words were hard to say, even to a stranger. The military had been my life for a long time.

"Lucas, what about this one?" Vash tugged on my belt to get my attention on her as she held up another shirt, this one blue with a fairy on it.

"Sure, that'll look great." Apparently, she was going to be able to blend in if she liked the kids' fashions that made no sense at all to me. When I'd been growing up on the family ranch in Wyoming, I'd always been wearing either classic cowboy plaid or solid blue or gray T-shirts and always with blue jeans. The only thing I ever wanted in the way of clothing had been a pair of cowboy boots, which I'd finally gotten when I was four.

Vash added the fairy shirt to the buggy. "Thanks." She moved on to the next rack.

Summers cocked his head. "I don't know what she is." He'd dropped his voice again.

"And this isn't the place to talk about it." Garnet shook her head. "Maybe we can find time somewhere to talk, but—"

"It's not her story to tell." I kept my voice level, not sure exactly what Brock was, and not wanting to start a fight in public. If he was anything like Agent Briar, he might get upset if I raised my voice, or got too defensive.

Summers nodded. "If you're going to be staying around, we should get together some time. We've got a place up in the mountains. Lots of critters. If you've been a critter person before, you'll need to learn how to get them comfortable around you again. I got lots of experience with it."

Yet another thing I'd not stopped to think about. How would a dog react to its human being furry from time to time? We'd always had a dog or three at the ranch, not to mention horses. If I wasn't going to be off fighting the next war, trying to save the world, would Vash like to have a dog or a pony? "Maybe, once we get settled, we can see. Guess this community I find myself in is larger than people make it sound."

"Not really." Summers shook his head and put his hands in his pockets. "You're just being lucky to run into a bunch of us. Garnet and Gavin are good folks. Stick with them." His phone rang. He pulled it out and glanced at it. "Need to take this." He turned away from us.

Garnet glanced in the buggy. "We're at seven shirts, how many are we going for?"

I touched the heavy red plastic of the buggy and shrugged. "No clue. Seven is a week, so maybe fourteen."

"Sounds like a good idea." Garnet smiled as Vash came back with a yellow shirt that had a few ruffles and buttons up the front.

"This one looks comfortable." Vash held it up so it was over her shoulders and down past her waist. "I like it. Will it fit?"

Garnet looked her up and down. "I think it will, sweetie. Let's find another six or so."

Vash beamed and put the shirt in the buggy. Then she hurried back over to the rack she'd been looking at.

Summers put his phone back in his pocket. "Need to go. Got a bear in a house up the mountain. I was hoping for a quiet day, but don't get many of those."

"Go on, keep the wildlife safe." Garnet grinned, then gave him a big hug.

He offered me another handshake. "Talk to you soon, Lucas."

I returned it and smiled. "Thanks. Nice meeting you." With Garnet's comment about the wildlife, I took a little closer look at Summers' badge. He was Colorado Parks and Wildlife. If he was some kind of shifter, that didn't match with what Agent Briar had told me about supernaturals not being part of public service. I wondered if Harris or Garnet might know the answers.

He headed out, and I glanced at Garnet. "Do you two need me for this? I'd like to pick up a few pairs of jeans and shirts. Most of my stuff is uniform or camo gear."

"Go ahead. Vash and I are having fun."

Vash came back with another shirt. "This one?"

I nodded. "Sure. Looks nice to me."

She added it to the cart and then hurried to find another one.

"Don't forget to get pants." I looked at the racks and shelves. "I know jeans, but got no clue on girl pants."

"Got you covered." Garnet looked like she wanted to laugh at me. "Go find your stuff, then we can see about shoes. I'll take care of underwear too."

"Shoes." I thought about Vash's feet. Her robes

were so long that I didn't remember seeing shoes or even her feet.

"She has slippers, but not shoes. We need a couple of different shoes for her."

"Garnet, thanks for coming along. There's so much I don't know about." How many trips would it take for me to go with Vash by myself for her shopping?

"Hey, no problem." Garnet grinned widely. "I'm loving this. Been a while since I took my niece shopping. They didn't always have the really cool kids' clothes when I was growing up, and fertility isn't something my kind are known for. I was amazed when I heard Cin and Chad had two daughters."

"You'll need to tell me more about that later." I was all about intel, and understanding why witches didn't have kids might be useful. "If anything happens, call and I'll be right back." I smiled a little. "Or you could scream. I'm good at running toward screams."

"I'll keep that in mind."

With a parting glance toward Vash who was heading back toward us with another shirt, I turned my focus to looking at the signs that would point me toward the men's wear.

The crowds were lighter there, and I relaxed as I started finding what I needed. As I shopped, I glanced around, trying to see if there was anyone strange around me. Agent Briar might claim there weren't a lot of supernaturals in Colorado Springs, but there sure seemed to be a lot of them around, and they all knew more than I did. By the time I found what I needed, and headed back toward Garnet and Vash, I'd worked myself up into a state where I was convinced everyone around me held a hidden life of somehow dancing naked under the full moon. Hopefully, as I learned more, I could force such ideas out of my head.

9

Despite the open country Agent Briar drove through, the traffic on the interstate was nearly bumper-to-bumper. It had been that way since we had gotten on the highway a short distance from Garnet's house. I wanted to try to find somewhere the traffic wasn't such a big issue and wondered how far away from Denver Vash and I would have to look to find a place that was at least mostly peaceful, somewhere I'd feel comfortable being able to protect her from things like effrits and other magical things I didn't even know about.

"Garnet's car moves fast, but not as fast as this." Vash stared out the window behind me. "It is amazing how much humans have done without magic. At least you keep telling me it's without magic."

"It is, Vash." I looked away from the tanker Briar was quickly approaching and into the backseat where she sat watching everything. "Or at least I presume it is. As I'm learning more, I guess it makes sense to ask if some of our more brilliant people weren't witches or something."

"Technically that's all *very* classified," Briar muttered without taking his gaze off the road. "But yes, a number of brilliant magic users and others have

86

shaped a large number of technological advancements over the years. That's not to say humans aren't responsible for a decent amount of it, but when you look at things like computers, you have to ask how someone came up with that one without knowing at least a little magic. Witches have been storing energy, memories, knowledge, and more in crystals for thousands of years."

Vash nodded, never taking her eyes from the window and the rolling landscape. "That is true. It's said that the first djinn was trapped in a piece of quartz before they figured out how to use brass and silver. I think that would be most cramped and uncomfortable. We might not be totally solid while we are inside the item we're bound to, but having some room to move around makes it easier. Lamps, bottles, bells, boxes, all of those are so much easier to exist in than things like swords and crystals."

"Swords?" I stared at her for a moment then looked at Briar. "Djinn can inhabit swords?"

"Sure." Briar huffed as he passed a slow-moving cattle truck. "You've heard of Excalibur, haven't you? That's a sword with a spirit tied to it. I don't know if it's a djinn, but it's a spirit. We've done some experiments trying to take some terminally ill people and catching their souls before they can go on and binding them to swords and such. I don't think the witches have it totally worked out since most of the time the souls go crazy after a while."

"Djinn and our kin are the only ones who can be safely bound to items." Vash turned away from the window and stared at Agent Briar. "How is it that you've forgotten such things? People of my time knew that and would never try something so horrible. Good people anyway." She pursed her lips and turned back to the window.

"The church and their like have done a good job of taking a lot of the knowledge of magic and locking it away." Briar looked a little uncomfortable and the mention of the church and I couldn't tell if he was referring to the Catholic Church or Christianity in general.

Vash shook her head, sending a shower of sparks that died before they reached the leather seat. "The gods should encourage curiosity in their followers. The djinn know this, as do those who dwell Underhill and in the other dimensions."

"Underhill?" Again, I looked from Vash to Briar.

Briar sighed. "You're going to need to curb some of your questions when you meet with Mark. He's open-minded, but a little old-fashioned when it comes to things like that. But Underhill. You've heard of elves, fairies, dwarves, and such, right?"

"Right." I didn't roll my eyes, but thanks to movies and books, everyone knew what an elf or dwarf was.

"Underhill is the term for the realm they come from. Truthfully, it's my understanding that it's a generic term for a bunch of pocket dimensions that are separated from Earth by a magical barrier." Briar gripped the steering wheel tight as he hit the brakes to avoid hitting an idiot on a crotch rocket who whipped in front of us for a second before angling toward the first exit to reach Castle Rock. The traffic was picking up, slowing down, and several other drivers hit their horns as the guy and motorcycle barely missed them on his journey across the lanes of traffic.

"There's a lot you're going to be learning over the next few years, Lucas." Briar hit the gas before the truck behind us pushed him down the road. "Most of it's going to be things werewolves never bother with, but if you're going to understand everything Vash has to offer, you're going to need to know more than the average new shifter. I guess it's a good thing Harris showed up when he did. He's a good man, even if he does get under my skin." He turned and glared at me for a moment. "Don't you dare tell him I said that."

I gave him a short salute. "I've got you." It was hard to bite back the smile that threatened to spread across my face. Most of my higher-ups in the Rangers would've died before letting anyone know they were being irritating. Things like that, I totally understood.

Vash's eyes widened and she looked at me. "Lucas, there are people for miles and miles. When we were traveling across the plains, I could sense some of them, but not in this number. How do you not drown in the feeling of them all?"

"We don't feel them all." I shook my head. "If I did, I might go crazy." Even knowing they were all out there, it was enough to make me feel them all pressing in on me. "If it's too much, you can retreat to your bell." I didn't want to command her back into her small metal prison, but both she and Harris had said it was comfortable and familiar to her. Honestly, I wished there was a way to free her from it. It didn't feel right that her life or her ability to experience life was tied to it and me.

"No," Vash whispered and shook her head. "I want to see it all. I can keep them at bay, like I do the effrits who are searching for me." It had taken Harris and Garnet some time to explain to her how to shield herself from the effrits. Their magic worked differently from hers, and even though she had absorbed English from me, some concepts didn't translate easily.

I reached over the seat and patted her arm. "Okay. But it's okay if you get overwhelmed and need to."

She gave me a weak smile. "Thank you, Lucas. I appreciate that you're not forcing me back to my bell. Never before have I had such freedom when someone has held my bell."

"People, even djinn, shouldn't be controlled by others." I sighed and faced the ever-increasing traffic as Briar cleared the town and started up the next hill.

As we got quiet, I wondered what the effrits would do to Vash if they got their bony hands on her. Briar and May didn't know much about them, and Vash didn't understand why they were after her, except that effrits consumed djinn when they could, devouring them and remaking them into something dark and deadly. I didn't want that to happen to Vash. The higher djinn, or whatever he'd been, had tasked me with guarding her, and I intended to do just that. Without the Army, it gave me a purpose and kept me from getting washed away I the newness of everything around me.

Agent Briar took an exit before we'd gone too far into the clogged arteries of Denver. "Okay, Lucas, even if I hadn't called him to let him know we were coming, Mark will feel us coming."

I scratched the short beard I'd decided to grow. It wasn't much, but it was a change from my life in the Rangers, where I'd had to be clean-shaven and looking perfect as much as possible. "Is he magical?"

"Yes and no. He's not a wizard, but the magic of being an alpha lets him claim territory and he knows any time a wolf passes through his boundaries. Since neither of us are bound to him, we'll feel like invaders. Don't be surprised if he isn't a little gruffer than I've been, or than Chad was."

"But I thought Kilkari was one of his wolves." Rank and file, wolves were going to be just like the military.

"He is, sort of." Briar stopped for a light. "I asked Mark to take Chad in to help him deal with things, since there wasn't an alpha down in the valley, and I didn't think the alpha in Albuquerque would be a good match for Chad. At this point, since Mark technically claims all of Colorado, Chad is like an old English lord, overseeing the southern valley for Mark. He might even be able to sense when wolves, and to a lesser extent other shifters, enter the area."

"Is there a possibility that I'll develop that wherever we settle?" I wasn't sure if I wanted 'control' of an area outside the land I wanted to own.

"Depends on if there's another wolf in the area, and how Mark feels about it." Briar took off from the light. "I'm not going to get involved in it. That'll totally be between you and Mark."

"Okay." I nodded and was a little amazed as the close-together houses fell away and more open areas appeared, some complete with barns and livestock.

"One of the big things to remember, and I know I've mentioned this several times since we left Kabul, but don't look superior wolves in the eyes." Briar flipped on his blinker and turned onto a narrow street that was paved, but barely wide enough for two cars. "They'll take that as a challenge, and I don't know what would happen to Vash if something happened to you."

Vash reached over the seat and patted my shoulder, much the same way as I'd been doing hers. "Please, Lucas, I don't want anything to happen to you. You're a good man."

I couldn't help but smile. "I'll do my best, Vash."

The driveway Agent Briar pulled into was like the drive of a country estate, but we were in the middle of the city. The wrought-iron gate was open and a neat half hedge ran along the driveway until the gravel opened up to a small parking area that already had a couple of trucks and Jeeps parked next to a small Tesla.

"There're four werewolves here." Vash glanced around. "One is following us from the gate."

Briar nodded as he parked next to the Tesla. "Don't let them know everything you can do. Hide your sparks, please."

Vash nodded, and the tingle I'd begun to understand was magic, danced over my skin as her hair seemed to lose some of its gloss and the sparks vanished. "Is this better?"

"Yes." Briar turned and smiled. "Stay quiet as possible, this is werewolf business."

"And everyone else was busy too," Vash muttered. "You explained that before we left Garnet's house."

"Okay, just so we're all on the same page." Agent Briar undid his seatbelt and opened his door.

I followed his lead, then opened the backdoor for Vash. The rental sedan was different from the Jeep we'd originally borrowed from the base. It reminded me of the things I didn't like in most cars, and that I was going to need to find myself a vehicle soon, probably a truck or SUV that I'd feel comfortable in.

Inside me, the wolf growled and the urge to turn and see who was stalking us rose up, but I focused on Briar as we ascended the half dozen brick steps up to the house. A pair of wolf statues stood at the top of the stairs where it met with a sprawling porch.

Vash took my hand. "Another wolf approaches. He's powerful." There was a bit of fear in her tone, and I squeezed her hand, trying to be comforting.

I resisted the urge to turn toward the werewolf I felt coming.

Agent Briar stopped a couple of feet from the front door and turned to the right where an average-looking man strolled toward us. He looked a little sweaty, like he'd just finished a jog. He paused at a round table that had the same metal design as the gates and picked up a white hand towel that he wiped across his face.

"Mark." Agent Briar stopped still, his face

toward the other wolf, but not looking him in the face.

My first impression of him was that he was someone I could easily take in a fight, but the wolf inside me wasn't so sure. Quiet power rolled off Mark, and I wasn't sure that was a power I wanted to mess with.

Doing the best I could, I followed Briar's lead as we faced the alpha who controlled Denver and all of Colorado. I stayed quiet as the two faced off. Power flowed between them, unseen, but tangible to everyone nearby. Even the wolf who'd followed us along the driveway, hidden by the short hedges, had to sense it.

Then Mark inclined his head ever so slightly. "Let's take a look at this pup you've brought me, Agent Briar. If he's as capable as the last one you dragged to my door, I may let you start recruiting when I need new pack members."

Agent Briar smiled a little tighter than normal, but he'd been telling me to not flash teeth at another werewolf, or it, like meeting their gaze, could be interpreted as a challenge, or warning. "Chad's a good man. I wanted him to find direction I couldn't provide. You've done well by him, and I hope Sergeant Lucas here will be another such wolf."

Mark looked me up and down.

The feelings inside me wanted to drop low to my belly and do everything possible to please him. Instead of following my wolf's lead, I squared my shoulders but didn't meet his gaze.

"Sergeant, Army Ranger from what Briar told me on the phone." Mark put his towel back on the table and took a couple of steps toward me. "Your wolf is young, so maybe, just maybe we can come to an understanding about who's in charge without too much conflict."

"I don't want any trouble." I was used to looking at people I spoke to, so not seeing his eyes made me uneasy. "If I could do this on my own, I would. But Agent Briar doesn't think that's possible."

"It often isn't, depends on the individual. Most new werewolves don't survive long without a pack around them. The urge to hunt is too strong, and since most people live in cities nowadays, the only thing there to really hunt is people. Hunting people will get you killed. Remember that. Chad was a special case in that regard. My first rule to all my pack, and the other shifters around Colorado. Humans aren't prey. Break that rule and I will personally hunt you down and put an end to you. Take out another wolf, we'll talk, but normally I put you down for that. From there, vampires and some of the fey are things we'll talk about. Deer, elk, bison—" he waved toward the hedges, "—those are fair game. We'll all share in the feast."

I nodded. "Understand." I reverted to speaking like he was a superior in the Army, it was easier to make the leap and know how I was supposed to act, well, other than not looking him in the eyes.

"Good." Mark paused and sniffed. "The child, she's not human. Smoke and cinders. She doesn't belong here."

"She's a bit of a complication." Agent Briar put a hand on Vash's shoulder. "Perhaps we could talk about her inside."

Mark shook his head. "I've had visits from her kind recently. Took me almost a day to get the stink out of the place."

A chill went through me. "Her kind?"

Mark frowned. "They didn't identify themselves, some kind of spirit creatures. Two of them. Looking for a girl and the wolf protecting her. Briar, once again you bring trouble to my land."

"Because I know you can deal with it." Again, Agent Briar turned up the edges of his mouth. "Do you still have that witch on staff? Persephone, if I recall."

"I do, and she went over the place thoroughly, said she hadn't ever encountered their kind before."

"Have her get in touch with Gavin Harris down in the Springs." Agent Briar took a breath, sounding like he was doing his best to not escalate the situation that had grown more tense than I'd hoped my first meeting with Mark would be. "He's got some information on the effrits we've been dealing with. Vash here isn't one of them, but something close."

"I don't mean any harm." Vash stepped between us toward Mark. "Lucas is my guardian."

"Guardian." Mark looked at me, then Briar. "I presume there's a story here."

"There is," Briar said before I could. "And not one that needs to be spoken out of doors."

Mark nodded slowly. "From the beings who were here two days ago, I agree. Persephone assures me that my home is secure from any prying eyes or ears." He skirted around Briar and approached the front door.

A muscular man ran toward him, pulling on a black T-shirt as he came. "Here, Mark, let me."

From his hasty appearance and obvious recent nudity, I presumed this was the wolf Vash and my wolf had sensed along the driveway. Why had he opted to reveal himself? If he'd waited until we entered the house, he could've come in without drawing attention to himself. Maybe he was wanting to make a bit of a show for my sake. He appeared in very good shape in his human form. It might have been his not-so-subtle way of telling me I'd be in for a fight if I tried to take him on. It probably wouldn't be in the best form to tell him I was in better shape than he was, and was used to being around guys with more muscles.

"Thank you, Robbie." Mark stepped aside as we followed him into the marble hallway. "Now, why don't you continue to patrol? I don't want any more surprises like the other day."

Robbie bowed slightly. "Yes, Sir." When we'd all cleared the door, he closed it again, remaining outside himself.

"My beta." Mark walked toward a room just off the entry. "He's new to the position and eager to please me. Sometimes too eager."

"New explains it all." Agent Briar took a seat across from the large, heavy desk.

"I think I'd have preferred Chad Kilkari to have the position, but he didn't want to move here to

Denver, and I can understand that. My previous beta was killed during an attempted takeover of my territory a couple of years ago, while I was out of the country for an alpha conference in Switzerland." Mark sat on the corner of his desk. "Luckily the vampires dealt with the problem before I returned home. Robbie was the highest-ranking wolf I had left, and Chad wasn't willing to fight him for the position."

"So, werewolf ranking is always accomplished by fighting?" It matched what Briar had told me, and I didn't see any reason to doubt him, but it was nice to have the intel confirmed by a second source.

"We have a lot of training to do with you, Sergeant Lucas." Mark blew out a long breath. "But first, explain this little girl to me. No one's going to overhear us. You can speak freely." Then he looked at Briar. "I presume she isn't a national secret or anything like that."

"To an extent." Briar spread his hands in a neutral gesture. "We don't want everyone to know about her, but there's already people looking for her, and none of them are human."

"Those effrits you mentioned." Mark tapped his desk. "I told them I didn't like unannounced supernaturals in my territory and they were welcome to leave as soon as they could."

"If they're asking for your help in finding her, then our efforts to block them must be working," Agent Briar leaned back in his chair. "That at least is good news."

"But you aren't answering my questions, Briar.

What is the girl?" There was enough of a growl in Mark's question that my inner wolf shrank back from him and the desk.

Since there were only two chairs in front of the desk, I motioned for Vash to sit on my knee. Her weight there was strange, but she seemed comfortable having a connection to me, and her presence there seemed to give the wolf inside me a sense of comfort.

"I am a djinn, or genie if you prefer." Vash squared her narrow shoulders and glared at Mark. Magic rolled off her and her dulled hair flamed to life, sending sparks cascading down like tiny comets. "A power greater than I entrusted Sergeant Lucas with me and he must keep me safe from the effrits who are seeking me."

Mark eased back in his chair, his eyes wide. "Interesting. I would've said some kind of elf, but elves don't have hair like yours, even the most powerful ones. Can't say as I've crossed paths with a djinn before, unless you count those effrits the other day. From the general feel, I'd say they are the darker side of your light."

"That's right," Briar drew attention back to himself. "We're still trying to get as much intel as we can, but at the moment, all we know is what Vash has told us, and what Gavin Harris has."

"So, Gavin knows about her." Mark pursed his lips and nodded slowly. "Then it's only a matter of time before the witches here in Denver do as well. Shortly after that, it'll be out to the vampires. Our community is fairly tight, even with the hour's travel between us. I've been thinking it would be a good idea to have one of my wolves in the Springs, the small pack in the mountains west of there is a specialty pack, and Brock Summers doesn't answer to me, so I need eyes there. Are you planning on staying down there?"

"There are resources down there that I can make use of," I replied, not totally caring to go into the details of a smaller VA office and other military benefits the Springs would easily provide that Denver couldn't. But like everything else in the larger city, it would be awkward and slower.

"Then *if* you survive your first shift, we'll see about setting you up down there. Gavin can introduce you around." The way he said it, Mark didn't have complete confidence in me coming through my first change intact. I hoped he was wrong, for Vash's sake as much as my own.

11

We had just gotten back on the interstate, heading south toward Colorado Springs, when Vash straightened in her seat with a loud intake of air.

I spun around and looked at her. "What's wrong, Vash?"

"An effrit. There's one coming toward us." She looked out the window toward the western sky, or maybe the mountains. "There."

"Where?" I turned the other way so I could see out my own window. A semi with a huge trailer moved past us, blocking my view for a moment.

"Aren't you shielding?" Briar glanced around as if trying to figure out what his next move should be.

Vash nodded. "Just like May and Garnet showed me. It shouldn't be able to sense me." She bit her lower lip. "I must be doing something wrong."

I patted her arm. "Or there could be another answer. Keep doing what you're doing."

Briar thrust his phone at me. "Call May. Tell her what's going on and that we might need help. With luck, this thing is just canvassing the area and we're in its path."

"Right." I knew from experience that sometimes the bad guys just managed to stumble across the good guys by accident, although given the last place they had seen us, it didn't make sense that they would be searching an hour away. It had been several days since we'd last dealt with them. It had been less time since Mark and the pack had met them.

As we cleared the semi-trailer, and I pulled up Briar's contact list, a shimmer appeared in the sky. It was little more than a heat distortion, like waves on the horizon in the desert. The effrit, it had to be. In seconds, I found Agent May's number and tapped to call it.

"Yeah, Boss, what's up?" She answered after the first ring.

"It's Lucas, we've got an effrit tracking us down the highway in Denver."

"An effrit? How did it find you?" Her voice went from slightly bored to excited.

"No clue. Vash just picked up on it and it's flying right at us." The heat shimmer was growing closer and closer.

"Water, they can't track you on or near water," May advised.

"And where is any water around here?" I'd seen people towing boats behind their big trucks, but hadn't seen more than a couple of small playa lakes on the trip into Denver.

"Give me a moment." The sound of fingers dancing across a keyboard came through the phone.

I pulled out my phone and asked where the closest lake was to our current location. It gave me two options, both along a highway. "Get off and turn around." I pointed to the next exit sign that was nearly a mile away.

"We'll be heading closer to it," Briar complained as he changed lanes, heading toward the exit.

"It's getting closer but slowed down." Vash still had her face against the window. "I don't think it's able to get a clear image of me with everyone else around."

"Lost in the herd." I nodded. "Do you think hiding under an overpass would help?"

"It's an effrit, not a hail storm." May huffed on the other end of the phone. "Looking at the roads and not just cross points, I think Chatfield Lake is your best bet. It's got fewer stoplights between the highway exit and the park. I'll make a couple of calls and get the way cleared for you."

Briar swung the car through the turn under the highway and back toward the northbound ramp. "Careful what you tell them, May, we don't need lots of locals getting in the way."

For a second, I saw the way the effrits back in Afghanistan had torn through the remainder of my unit. Local first responders wouldn't be equipped to deal with even one effrit. I wanted to tell Briar to head toward somewhere there weren't many people and maybe Harris, May, and some of the other magical community could meet us there and take the effrit out before innocents could be caught in the crossfire, but I didn't think we were ready for that yet.

"I know what I'm doing, Boss."

I zoomed my phone search in for Lake Chatfield. "I've got the route. Take the second exit. Why does it say construction?"

"There's always construction," Briar muttered. "One of the first rules of chasing bad guys."

After a second, I decided to not point out that the bad guy was chasing us. "Vash, is there anything you can do?" I looked out the window, but the trip under the highway had made it hard to locate the effrit's vague distortion in the sky.

"He might feel my magic if I try," Vash frowned. "I am sorry, Lucas. I wish there was more I could do, but it is too far for me to teleport you and Agent Briar back to Garnet's home, and the vehicle is too heavy for me to move even a slight distance."

I gave her a soft smile, hoping it was something she'd understand meant that I didn't blame her for not being able to help.

"Hey, what about a parking garage?" May suggested. "Would the metal mess with their magic?"

Again, Vash shook her head. "I don't believe so. All djinn have different weaknesses, and metal, particularly iron, affects me, but the effrits would most likely be undeterred by it. They are creatures of fire, so water is a good idea."

"It was just an idea, and a good one." I felt a little pang as we sped past a huge parking structure that looked like it was part of the parking for the light rail system.

"Take the exit for the loop." I pointed to the sign that indicated west and east possibilities.

"On it." Briar gave the car a little more gas and we sped past a quartet of leather men on motorcycles.

"There it is." Vash looked out the back window and pointed. "It's like it can't see me, exactly, but knows what it's looking for."

Wishing I could see what she was watching, I looked at my phone and it said we were still several minutes from the lake.

"Tell her to keep her shields up," May instructed. "If it can't see you exactly, then it might be following the car somehow. Luckily white sedans are popular in the Denver area, so maybe you can scrape it off on another sedan."

I reached back and tapped Vash's shoulder. "Could you hear May?"

"Yes, and she could be correct."

"But how would it know to follow the car?" Briar cleared the ramp to the new highway and sped up again. "That doesn't make much sense. Do they even know what cars are?"

"If they haven't been imprisoned inside something like Vash was, and have been part of the modern world, then how could they not? They have cars and trucks in the Middle East." I glanced at my phone; we still had several exits to go before the lake. Luckily, we weren't in the middle of a rush hour and the going through the construction was fairly smooth.

Briar shook a finger at me. "You've got a point there, Lucas." We drove next to a white sedan that was exiting. As soon as it wasn't a viable option, Briar headed toward the next one in sight.

Vash turned from the window. "It followed the other car for a moment. Is this what you wanted?"

"Yes. I was hoping to confuse it." Briar paced the next white sedan.

"Then I might be able to help. It is just a small

magic, and maybe the effrit won't feel it, or be so confused by it that it won't be able to focus in on me." Vash smiled slightly.

Her hair sparked as the magic flowed out of her. The hair on my arms stood on end at the touch of magic, then it was gone.

"Crap." Briar hit the steering wheel. "Did you just make every car on the highway white?"

"That does give us more cover, does it not?" Vash looked confused.

Briar nodded. "It does, I just wish I'd thought of the idea first."

I couldn't argue with Briar on that. It was a great idea. "What happens when those people realize their cars are white and not the color they bought?"

"It will fade in a day." Vash looked a little pleased with herself as her hair went back to the flatter tones she used to hide her sparks. "Most djinn magic doesn't last long. Things made with magic fade in a day. Some of the older djinn can make permanent things, but that costs us our life energy."

"So, you couldn't make us a house, and have it still be there the next day?" That would save us a lot of time and money if she could.

"Magic doesn't work that way, Sergeant," May said through the still open phone connection.

"May is right." Vash looked back out the window. "There are limits to what magic can do. The effrit is still following, but it's having trouble finding us. It is looking in each conveyance."

"Good. Here's our exit." Briar broke off from the pack of white cars. Three other cars came with us.

"Although we might have some difficulty getting the car over the lake."

"There's a bridge you can stop on," May advised. "The park gate has been told to open for the next few minutes and not stop anyone from coming in. You should be able to go through without delay."

"Thanks, May, you're awesome." Briar turned toward the park entrance.

"The effrit just passed over us." Vash looked up as we passed under the highway.

"Then it's still checking out the other white cars." I let out a little breath, but was determined to not totally relax until we knew the way was completely clear.

"I think so." Vash craned her neck around like she was trying to see what was happening back on the highway. "I can no longer see it."

"I don't know if we should stick with the plan, or make a run for the Springs." Briar drummed on the steering wheel.

"Since we don't know how it's tracking us, let's stick with the plan." The lake was visible as we drove toward the park entrance. I hoped we'd be so far away that the effrit wouldn't be able to locate us.

"There's another one coming." Vash leaned over the seat and looked out the front window. She pointed toward a heat distortion heading our way.

Briar nodded and turned into the park. "Right. Bridge it is."

I wondered how long we'd be able to park on the bridge before the humans got irritated with us, probably not long. "Vash, if we're over the water, where the effrit won't be able to sense us, could you change the color of our car?"

She smiled slyly. "Sure. That would be easier than changing the other cars."

"And if the magic doesn't last long, we don't have to worry about changing it back before I return the car with it being the wrong color." Briar nodded. "I like the way you think, Lucas."

"The best military training in the world." I wondered if the pain of not being in the Army would go away. Vash was my unit now. Briar and May weren't going to be around long, just a few more days, getting me through my first full moon, and helping us find a long-term place to live. Until we found more people like Harris, we were going to be on our own. It felt lonely, even with the idea that I might be part of Mark's pack.

The bridge came up quickly and Briar parked there just long enough for Vash to turn the car from white to black, then we took off again, avoiding the interstate and heading south toward Colorado Springs and the safety Garnet's house provided.

12

"I just want you to understand I don't know the market up here as well as I do the one in the valley, but Cin and Chad said to see what I can do to help out." The slightly heavy Hispanic woman across Garnet's kitchen table from me was Marzie Campbell, an associate of the Kilkaris. She'd come to Colorado Springs to help find a place for me and Vash. "You're looking for a single-family home; do you want it in the city, or on some property?"

Cities always felt cramped and confining, and I didn't really want to put people in danger from things like effrits. As much as I hoped they wouldn't always be a problem, I'd seen enough fighting to know there were normally people willing to step up and keep the struggle going, unless you made a major impression on them. "Some property, I think."

"Do you have any ideas on where? There're lots of listings all around the area that will put you outside the Springs, but close enough to enjoy what the city has to offer." Marzie started tapping on her keyboard.

"I'm going to be spending a few days a month up in Denver."

Marzie nodded. "Yeah, Chad mentioned you were going to be pack mates. So maybe somewhere north of Colorado Springs, but still close enough for the VA and base access." Her fingers flew across the keys. "What can you afford? Are we getting you a VA loan, traditional loan, or are you paying cash?"

"Depends on what we find, but I think I'd prefer to pay cash." For years, I'd put most of my checks in the bank, and at times my hazard pay had been fairly hefty. In my mind, I'd been shooting for being a lifer, and wanted to wait until I ended up behind a desk before buying a house. That thought also reminded me I was going to have to figure out what I was going to do for an income. Sure, I was going to get retirement, and it was going to be a decent amount, but there was no way I was going to sit around watching soap operas and taking care of Vash. I had to have something to do.

"Okay, cash will help us keep the turnaround time low. We can put in a bid, then just let your bank talk with their bank and transfer the funds. What's your top-level amount you want to pay?"

"Keep it around five hundred K and we should be fine."

"Good. I should be able to find something with that. Might be a little ways from the city, and not huge."

I held up my hands. "It's just going to be the two of us, so we don't need a lot of room in the house. Land…see what we can find." Growing up on the ranch, I liked the idea of land, and the more of it we had the less chance there was that a neighbor might see or hear something odd that attracted attention.

Marzie smiled as she worked. "Do you mind a

fixer-upper? I know good people who can help, people who you wouldn't have to hide around."

"I'm good at killing people. It's been years since I built anything useful." Mending fences in high school wasn't the same as making a run-down house livable.

"Then we'll start looking for move-in-ready houses." Marzie looked up. "Let me make a couple of calls and see if we can look at a couple today."

Harris strolled in, holding Vash's hand, and frowned. "We might want to put that off a few days."

"Why?" As the word left her lips, Marzie's eyes widened in understanding. "Oh, yeah. Control."

Letting go of Harris' hand, Vash looked at me. "I can help with that."

"How?" I was getting tired of not getting the things everyone else around me understood on an almost instinctive level.

"Djinn can have a calming influence on others." Vash smiled and her hair glowed and sparked.

My chest loosened as a wave of relaxation washed over me. I felt better than I had in days. There wasn't even the hint of the wolf deep inside me. It was like when I'd been in the hole where the effrit and light being had fought and the chime had rung out. Vash's bell had been there, and she'd used her magic then to help me relax.

"If we wait, will it be easier to get something set up so we can find something fast? I don't want to wear out our welcome here." I ran my hand over Vash's hair, sending more sparks cascading toward the floor. Even after a few days, I still expected her hair to be warm and burn me as the sparks flew out of it, but it wasn't. To me, it was an example of her magical being. I'd seen fathers touch their children's hair like that and hoped the gesture was comforting to her.

"You're not going to wear out your welcome." Garnet appeared in the door to the kitchen. "I like having the two of you around. Vash lights up the place."

Vash smiled. "You're very nice, Garnet. Your light is strong."

"Thank you. That means a lot coming from you." Garnet bent slightly and hugged Vash.

"What do you think, Gavin, would two days, or three after the moon be long enough?" Marzie had stopped typing and was watching us.

Harris spread his hands and shrugged. "I'm not a werewolf, but I've dealt with a few of them over the years. Two days should be plenty… as long as his first shift goes smoothly. Every wolf is different, and we won't know until he gets through it."

"I'm standing right here, Harris." I tried to not sound snarly, but even with the calming Vash had done, it came through. I didn't like not having more control over myself. "You can talk to me."

"Sorry, Lucas, sometimes I fall into teaching mode." Harris kept his eyes low, like he was trying to avoid challenging me.

Taking a deep breath, I forced the edge of anger down. "Understood." I turned my attention back to Marzie. "Sounds like it'll be good to go in three days. See what you can set up and we'll start looking."

Closing up her laptop, Marzie grinned. "Sounds like a plan. I'll spend the next couple days making some phone calls and setting up showings. You're Army, so I presume you're an early riser."

I bit back a chuckle. "Maybe one of these days, I'll be able to sleep past six."

"Then I'll arrange a hotel room, so we can get an early start." She tucked her computer in her bag. "Hope your moon goes smoothly."

"Thanks for coming." I nodded to her. I still wasn't sure why she'd driven three hours to come, particularly since we hadn't spent a ton of time going over properties.

"Any time." She turned toward the door. "I know what it's like to be new to the supernatural community."

Seconds later, the door closed and she was gone.

"I like her." Garnet leaned against the back of the chair Marzie had deserted. "Not sure what her gifts are, but she's got potential."

"And we're not going to upset Cin by stealing her understudy." Harris took a seat at the head of the table.

Vash straightened and frowned. "They're close."

Harris put his hands on the table and closed his eyes. "You're right." His voice was soft and sounded far away.

Doing my best to stifle a growl, I put my hand on Vash's shoulder.

Garnet tapped the table slowly. "They aren't pushing on my shields."

"But they are close." Harris opened his eyes. "It's

like they're doing a grid search for us. I wouldn't have expected something like that from them."

A grid search was something I could understand. Over the years, I'd done plenty of them with my unit, trying to flush out terrorists. "Everyone just stay still. No magic. Maybe they'll pass us by again. Movement… magic will give us away." A frustrated growl welled up out of me. "We've got to figure out some way to take these guys out, or get them to leave us alone."

"They are effrit," Vash whispered. "There are limits to what they can do, just like there are limits to what I can do."

"We've all got limits." I looked at Vash and didn't like the fear on her face. "But I think you're trying to say if we can work with their limits, we can find a way to deal with them."

She nodded.

"And I've got people reaching out to people who might know," Harris said in a more normal voice. "But they have to be careful or the effrits will figure out we're trying to get information. Briar is also trying to get his intel network working for us."

I hoped the information would come soon so we could move against them. "Unfortunately, Briar's network doesn't sound as connected as yours."

"Because magical people are good at sniffing out feds, and spies." Harris laughed. "Luckily, there's a few people over there who don't like the things the Taliban and their ilk are trying to do and are willing to work with some of us."

"But you aren't officially part of Briar's group."

I pointed out.

"Right, but that doesn't mean we can't be working for the greater good." Harris stood and strode into the kitchen. "You see, a lot of people aren't gung-ho about how governments operate, but still want to make sure the bad guys don't take over the world. When you work in the shadows of the shadows, things can get rather dark rather quickly." There was the creak of the fridge opening and closing followed by the pop of a soda can being opened seconds before Harris returned with sodas for all of us. "Besides, as good as Briar's team is about dealing with supernatural threats that originate here on Earth, I doubt they'd be much use handling things coming from other dimensions."

Shaking my head, I held up my hands. "I don't even want to go there yet. Too steep of a learning curve as it is. Once I've got all the intel from here on Earth, then we can learn about other places."

Vash's face relaxed. "They've moved on."

"But their scans are getting more frequent and concentrated." Garnet took her soda and opened it. "We might want to think about going elsewhere, your house, Gavin, that's fairly well protected."

"Yeah, and it's also in the middle of town," Harris objected.

"Then figure out how to deal with them, and we can all relax." I opened my soda and downed half of it. It would be so nice if I could just break out a large gun and shred the effrits, but that wasn't going to happen. "Magic bullets." I snapped my fingers. "Can you guys make magic bullets?"

Harris' face lit up. "Now why didn't I think of that? I might know just the person for that." He glanced at the clock. "Be we probably won't be able to get in to see him until tomorrow, and he's in Denver."

"Then it's a good thing we're going to Denver tomorrow." I wondered if I would be able to handle talking to someone about magical bullets the next day, or would the moon be too close? We'd have to see. If I'd stumbled onto a possible answer to our problem, I'd do my best to hold back the wolf until I was done. Magic bullets might be the answer I needed.

13

From the looks of the metal shop we pulled up into, Digger's Cave, it wasn't the most savory neighborhood in Denver. The place had razor wire around the top of the chain-link border fence and a number of broken-down cars, apparently being parted out, were scattered around haphazardly.

Harris had made the phone calls, but since Briar, Kilkari, and I had an appointment with Mark and the pack in a few hours, he'd stayed behind. Briar assured him that he was familiar with Digger Urson.

"I still can't believe I didn't think of this earlier. Urson's the best magical smith in the country." Briar pulled up to the curb outside the gate. "He can create nearly any magical weapon you can need."

"And tools," Kilkari said from the backseat. "He's good at tools too. I've seen some of his work in those… well, and a nice sword he did for a friend."

After years of dealing with terrorists who used as many homemade weapons as they did professional, I knew some very dangerous things could come from a competent weaponsmith. Somehow, it felt strange to walk into such a shop just east of Denver proper.

I scratched my arm as we got out of Briar's car. That morning I'd woken up itching and angry. It was hard to keep myself under control.

"Stop that." Briar frowned at me. "It's your wolf ready to come out. If you keep up the scratching you'll leave your arms and hands bloody before the moon rises this afternoon."

"This afternoon?" I jerked toward the eastern horizon. All that was there was the rise of the freeway, but I didn't know when the moon was going to rise. Didn't it always come up after dark? That's how all the books and movies showed it, but I could remember seeing the full moon in a blue sky.

"Closer to evening, than afternoon." Kilkari had stopped at the front bumper and was looking at me. "The full moon differs each month. We're not always lucky enough to have it be after dark, although when you stop and think about it, after dark adds a level of suspense for things like movies. Fiction and fact are often two different things."

A dark musky scent hit me, and as Briar and Kilkari turned toward the building, four huge, feral-looking men stalked toward us. They carried axes and long-handled hammers, looking like a squad of Vikings ready to sack an English village.

Reflexively I reached for a sidearm, but I hadn't carried one in almost a week. There wasn't anything modern weaponry could do to the effrit, and Briar had told me to leave things behind just to prevent civilian injuries. In that moment, I wondered if I hadn't made a major mistake by following Briar's lead.

"I thought they were expecting us." Kilkari stiffened and felt like he was ready to fight.

Briar held up his hand. "Both of you stand

down."

"Back off before I name you all mongrels." A voice bellowed across the beat-up ground between the shabby building and the fence where the four big men had stopped at the gate just a few feet from Kilkari.

The man who came stalking out was a good six foot seven, maybe nine, I couldn't be sure at the distance. He didn't carry any weapons, but danger rolled off him. His chest was nearly as broad as my shoulders and his arms looked like he could bend I-beams easily. His long blond beard mingled with the hair on his chest. "I told Gavin this was a bad idea. Wait a few days I suggested, but he wouldn't hear it." He pushed between the two men standing in the middle of the gate, and the way they stumbled away from him, he'd stopped himself from using his full strength and sending them flying. "But you should've known better, *Agent* Briar."

There was something odd in the way he accented the word agent, and I couldn't tell what since he had a slight European accent, Nordic, just shy of German.

"Harris was right; we don't have tons of time." Briar stomped over to him, and he looked like he was fighting with his own wolf who wasn't taking kindly to the big man and his underlings. "Urson, we need weapons. Harris said he'd sent you an email with the details."

Urson huffed. "I got it. But if I'm going to craft a true magical weapon, I'm going to need to meet the hands that are going to wield it. He said it wasn't for you, but a new wolf." He looked at Kilkari first, but then his intense gaze was weighing me.

The big man frowned. "Magic dances around you. I don't trust the fae, but your wolf struggles. You'd be Lucas. Come."

Briar started forward, but Urson held up his hand. "Just him. If you want a full-scale battle you can't win, Briar, then the three of you come onto my property. Even I couldn't stop my bears from ripping three wolves apart with the moon only a few hours from showing her face. I can protect one cub."

Briar straightened.

"Back down, Briar." Urson straightened and flexed his massive chest. It was probably a trick of light or something, but even more blond hair seemed to pop out of his skin. "You can't win here, and I don't care about that badge you wave around to bring others under your control. If you want a weapon capable of bringing djinn down, then I need to get to know the wolf who will wield it. You have my word, no harm will come to him, and I'll bring him back to you in time to reach Maxum's compound before the moon rises." He pointed at me. "Come. We're burning sunlight."

I glanced at Briar.

From the tight line of his lips and set of his suddenly heavy brows he was fighting saying or doing something we'd all regret. His nod was barely perceivable, but it was enough.

Without another word, I slowly walked over to Urson. When I crossed from the battered sidewalk onto the packed dirt of the work yard, magic tingled across my skin, like the shields Garnet kept around her house. A week earlier I wouldn't have known what it was, but knowing, I wondered what I was getting into.

"Come along, Lucas, we need to move quickly." Urson turned to start toward the building. He paused and glanced back at the four men standing at the gates. "I think the four of you have things to do before we lock up and break out the mead. The wolves are properly cowed, there's no need to worry about them."

Their stances didn't change much, but they turned from the gate and stalked back toward the stacks of metal they'd emerged from. The dangerous energy faded as they disappeared.

"I am sorry that circumstances do not make things easier for us." Urson resumed walking toward the building. "If this could've waited a while, my men wouldn't be on the edge they are today. You'll learn that the full moon brings out the worst in shifters, even those of us who are born to the fur. It's worse for you who have been turned without permission."

"People choose this?" I supposed it was possible, but it wasn't something I'd have gone along with if I'd been given a choice.

"Yes." Urson laughed and turned to me with a welcome smile. It brightened his face and made him look like a gentle giant. "I think, if you'd been given a choice, you'd have made a better bear than a wolf. We are the warriors of old, and you will always be a warrior, contrary to what the wolves will try to make you."

Returning his smile, I nodded. "Ex-army ranger."

"Tell me your story, Lucas." Urson walked into a room that had an ancient anvil in the center. On the far wall a massive forge stood, the coals glowed softly, hinting at the fire they were no doubt capable of. "Be quick, though, Briar isn't going to wait long and if he charges my gates he'll find a bigger fight than he wants. Your tale will help me craft the right weapon for you."

I stood straight and explained how the Afghan werewolves had attacked my unit, then how the effrits had finished them off.

Urson shook his head. "That's the recent part." He pointed at my chest. "Who is Sergeant David Lucas…no, better, who is David? Leave Sergeant Lucas behind, go back to your core. Who are your people? Where do you come from? Gavin asked me for a weapon capable of killing djinn, that's no small magic, and not one I'm willing to let out into the world easily. I need to know you."

"No." I shook my head. "I'm not trying to kill djinns, just effrits." I didn't want anything that might hurt Vash around the house.

Urson glared past me toward the gate where Briar and Kilkari leaned against the car looking like a couple of cops in an old TV show, waiting for an informant to come out and talk to them. "They haven't told you, have they?" He shook his head and a bit of metal fell out of his beard and clanked off the anvil.

"I'm having a huge learning curve with all of this, there's a lot they haven't told me." I was so sick of the learning curve and wished there was some way

Vash or May could just magic the information into my brain so I could stop feeling like I was half a mile behind everyone else with no hope of winning the race.

"Let me go back and put this into human terms. What's the difference between a European and an African?"

The question took me by surprise. Was he trying to determine if I was a racist? "They're all just superficial, at our cores we're all the same."

"They. They're all the same." Urson shook his head. "You're no longer human, well, if you survive the night. If not, none of it will matter. But you're right, and when you look at djinn and effrit, it's the same as looking at humans. At their core, they're the same. Sure, some of their differences are a bit more than skin deep. Their goals are vastly different, but beyond that, they're the same. What will kill an effrit will also slay a djinn."

My chest tightened. Was part of guarding Vash also going to be able to kill her if she became a threat? It wasn't something I liked to think about.

Urson put a heavy hand on my shoulder. "You are a good man, David. I can tell that, and the magic of my forge can as well. Don't think of the possibility of harming your young charge. I'll cast the weapons so only your hand can wield them. To anyone else, they will be just pretty paperweights."

"That's something," I muttered.

"It is." Urson patted my shoulder. "Now come on, give me your early years, what shaped you into the man you are today? You can do the cliff-notes version, Briar's not going to wait forever, and we can all feel the moon calling." A thoughtful look crossed his face. "Yes, I think her magic will be needed in this casting. Once my bear has had his fill, the magic will be strong."

It didn't make any sense to me, but I nodded and told him bits of my growing up on the ranch, of my family, as much as I dared. Sure, he knew my name, but I didn't give him family names. I only had Briar and Harris speaking for his trustworthiness.

"Loves?" Urson asked as I finished my tale.

Another question that took me by surprise. "I've never had time to love." It was the closest to the real truth I was willing to give him.

He pursed his lips and his blue gaze bore into me. After a moment, he ran a thick-fingered hand through his shaggy hair. "What do you love? When you have the chance, what makes your warrior's heart soften and slow? There's always something that helps us be quiet and brings us peace."

I stopped and pondered his question. It had been years since I'd felt at peace when I was awake. There was always another terrorist waiting behind the next building, aiming to shoot at me or my unit. Even when we were flying there was the chance someone would attempt to bring down the plane or helicopter. When we weren't actively fighting, there was staying on the alert when dealing with the strangers fixing our meals, or pouring drinks. It was hard to find a memory of being at true peace, of letting myself just relax. The last time had been the summer after I graduated high school, waiting to report to basic training. "Riding in the mountains in the summer when there's a storm coming in and the air is full of electricity."

Urson laughed. "You would make a great bear, Lucas. I know the weapons I need to craft for you. I'll enjoy sending Briar the bill for this one." He came around the anvil and held out his hand. "Let me see your hand."

Not sure I totally understood, I put my hand in his.

He turned it over and looked at my palm, then slowly curled my fingers to the position they'd be in if I held a sidearm. "Good. A large grip and wide guard. Something that won't add new calluses to you. I can do that." He looked at my arms. "Do you prefer a sword or an axe?"

"I don't know. Why?"

"Gavin found a spell, or part of a spell. I think I can finish it out for him. I've got my own witch working on it. If I'm right, it'll be another way to deal with the effrits, if my ideas for something more modern don't do the trick. The thing is, it has to be cast into a blade, so sword or axe? You have the build to swing either easily."

I'd never worried about ancient weapons. "Whatever you think is right. You're the weaponsmith."

Again, Urson laughed. "I like you, Lucas. I hope your little wolf survives his first night in the world. If it doesn't then my work will be for naught. Go on. I'll call Gavin… no, Briar, he's paying for all this, when it's ready. Probably this weekend sometime." He rubbed his hands together and grinned. "I'll add a rush charge to it, just to goose him a little harder. When you come back, bring your djinn, as she might be able to do a bit of extra magic on things to give them extra oomph."

"Okay." I wasn't sure exactly what to say. Deep inside me, the wolf wanted to snap at Urson as I turned and headed toward the car. He'd cowered under the bear's handling, but I felt the need to part with a nip or something to tell him I was more than just a thing he could touch as he saw fit. These were some of the strongest feelings I'd gotten from my wolf, and it was all I could do to keep it from showing. The itching grew stronger, and it was hard to not scratch.

"Go on, little cub," it sounded like Urson was talking to my wolf more than me. "Come back when the moon isn't pulling on us so strongly."

Taking it as a more formal dismissal, I smiled and nodded. "Thanks, Urson."

"You can call me Digger, and I'll call you David."

As I trudged back toward the car, I wasn't sure how I felt about him using my first name. It felt strange. He wasn't exactly a friend, yet, and he wasn't family. Time would tell.

Briar visibly relaxed as I approached the car. "About time. I was ready to come in there and get you. We need to get moving."

Kilkari nodded. "We've got just enough time. Urson was a bit more intimidating than I expected. RJ made him sound… more friendly."

I opened the back door. "He's friendly enough, just a bit on edge due to the moon."

"That's got us all on edge." Briar slipped behind the steering wheel. "Sorry you had to go through that today of all days."

"It's okay." I buckled myself in, feeling a little silly since, if they were telling me the truth, I couldn't die in a car crash unless there was silver in the vehicle. "But I did have the urge to snap at him as I left." I scratched my arm again as Briar pulled away from the curb. There was a lot I still needed to understand, and I hoped that by the time the sun rose, or the moon set, I'd be better equipped to handle the world that was changing around me.

14

By the time we pulled up to the gate near a hill that rose high even among the foothills west of Denver, the itching was so bad I was sitting on my hands, squirming like a teenager in the back seat. I was determined to keep myself under control even as I wanted to tear something apart. The sooner the better.

"We're cutting it close, Briar." Kilkari's voice was deeper than normal. It had been several minutes since any of us had spoken, and the roughness of his words hit me hard.

"Yeah." Briar didn't sound any different. He pulled out his phone and made a call. "We're here."

The gate swung open.

When I realized we were taking a different route from when we visited Mark before, Kilkari explained that the pack spent the full moon nights on his property outside of Evergreen, a town in the foothills just west of Denver. It sounded like a safer idea than having a bunch of wolves in an elite area of a big city.

Briar drove up the long driveway. There was a huge cabin at the end of the dirt trail. A dozen vehicles were already there. They were varied, showing the diversity of the pack. A beat-up truck sat next to a gleaming sports car, and on the other side of the truck was a Subaru with a soccer decal on the back window.

Excited energy rolled off Kilkari as we parked and he opened his door.

My itching got worse, and my hands were shaking so hard I could barely force myself to get out of the car. Even as I forced my hands into my jeans' pockets, I wondered if I was going to shred the thin fabric there in an effort to claw at my legs.

Mark stood on the sweeping wooden steps going up to the cabin. "Cutting it a little close, aren't you?" He was calm, but there was a disappointed edge to his tone. His flannel shirt was open revealing a muscular chest. Behind him, several other men stood, including Colfax, the beta who was stripped to just a pair of sports shorts. He had a more powerful build than Mark and looked more dangerous.

"Couldn't be helped." Briar looked defensive, but not as much as he had with the bears.

"Let's get out back; the others are already there." Mark turned toward the doors. "Drop your clothes wherever you want."

My hands shook as I pulled off my T-shirt. The itching backed off, like the wolf inside me knew it was about to be let out. I stopped at a chair just inside the living room and dropped the shirt there. It didn't take me long to yank off my boots and pants. I only gave a passing thought to being naked in front of strangers. Briar and Kilkari had warned me about it, and I was ready. What I wasn't ready for were the four wolves who came trotting toward us from the open patio doors.

Inside me, something shook. Wolves. I was supposed to become a wolf as the moon rose, but wolves had killed half of my unit.

"You're going to need to relax, Lucas…David." Mark took off his shirt and stood in front of me. "It'll be much easier if you relax and let your wolf come out as easily as possible."

His voice had a hypnotic quality to it. I shivered. My wolf pushed closer to my skin. The itching returned and I felt like I was getting hairier by the moment.

"It's okay, Lucas." Kilkari put a hand on my shoulder. His skin was almost burning hot.

Reflexively I rolled my shoulder, like I was trying to rub against his touch.

One of the wolves who'd come in, a large gray female, rubbed up against him, pushing her shoulder into his legs, causing him to bump against me for a moment.

My vision changed. Everything got too bright until I blinked and everything fell back to close to normal. Each of the wolves, both in fur and skin, glowed with a magical light. As my wolf pushed harder, I tried to relax and let him slip into my skin like I'd been told to do.

"That's right," Mark's voice still held a command, but it was soothing.

Fur brushed against my bare leg.

Unwillingly, my throat tightened. The sensation of fur on skin was something I'd felt before. Right before teeth tore into me. I pushed it back. I had to relax. Briar and Kilkari had told me if I didn't relax and just let the shift happen then it would be agonizing. Kilkari had said he'd fought his first change and had been in pain for days afterward.

My wolf surged, filling me with fur and freedom.

Somewhere nearby a wolf howled.

The wolves in the house lifted their muzzles and joined in the song.

The song. The howls.

Death.

The howls were what tore my unit apart. They were everywhere. The fur on my skin.

I didn't have a weapon. I had to get away. They were all around me. I lashed out. My fist hit someone. I couldn't tell who.

More howls erupted.

There were more coming.

Someone grabbed my arm.

I jerked back. I had to get away. There were too many.

Rifle fire erupted. Men screamed. The howls grew louder.

Someone was shouting my name.

Fire burned inside me. I couldn't give into the fire. The fire was part of the howls. The howls and fur killed my unit.

They had come in the sand. The howls were deep inside me. They drowned out the sound of the sandstorm that had birthed them.

Around me, the rest of my unit fired even as my finger reflexively squeezed my rifle's trigger. Shots went wide, only a few of them found solid targets.

The howls were enough to muffle sounds of gunfire. They wrapped around us, smothering us.

Men screamed. My men. My unit. Strong Army Rangers screamed. As the howls rang out, men screamed.

I was screaming. Fangs closed in on my arm, tearing my flesh from bone.

The pain seared through me. So much pain, so many howls that were louder than the gunshots and screams. They tore into us like nothing should be able. They killed my unit. How, why had I survived?

A chime rang in my head. The sound offered hope. Its purity eclipsed the howls and forced them away. Coolness welled up inside me and pushed the fire away.

"Sleep, Lucas," Vash's soft voice broke through the fur and fire. "You're safe now."

As the coolness chased the fire away, my wolf fled deep inside me, taking everything of me with it, leaving nothing in its wake. The darkness was welcoming silence.

"Easy there." Mark's tone was soothing as light returned. "How are you feeling?"

I blinked. Vash sat at my side, on the edge of a couch, and from the looks of it, we were still in Mark's cabin mansion. There were even still clothes scattered around, but there weren't any wolves there, except Mark and Briar.

"You're going to be okay, Lucas." Vash patted my hand. "I chased away your fears."

"My fears?" I blinked and even that little motion left me wanting to go back to sleep. "What happened?"

"That's a good question." Briar paced in front of a massive fireplace. His shirt was untucked, but on and buttoned.

Mark shook his head. "You don't understand broken people, do you, Briar? You're an alpha, can you even feel his wolf right now?"

Briar frowned. "No. That doesn't make sense. It was breaking through before he started screaming and punching people."

"Punching?" With a painful effort, I lifted my arm and looked at the knuckles of my left hand. There was new pink skin like I'd hurt myself and it had been long enough for them to heal.

"Yes." Mark came over and squatted just behind Vash. "Poor Chad's going to have a pretty good bruise when he returns to skin later. You were close enough to your shift that when you broke his jaw it was like if your wolf had attacked him. I helped him heal most of it with his shift to wolf, but he won't be eating any of the elk they brought down a little while ago."

"I hit Kilkari?" I remembered trying to get away from the hands on me. I hadn't had a sidearm. The howling. The howling had been like when my unit was attacked.

"You called out for help and I came." Vash's voice was soft like she was trying to soothe a younger child. "You'll come when I need you, too."

"Yes, I will." I patted her hand in turn. "I just

don't understand what happened."

"Since I have to make a guess, I'm going to say you've got PTSD." Mark stood and looked at Briar. "Maybe, if we'd gotten to you sooner after the attack, we'd have been able to figure this out before your first full moon."

Briar stopped pacing and glared at Mark. "I'm not a psychiatrist. How was I supposed to spot the signs?"

"Everyone with PTSD is different." Mark looked away from Briar. "Since he didn't spend any time around the pack before the moon, we had no way of knowing. Unless you and Chad have been shifting and howling around him."

A huff escaped Briar. "Like we've had time for things like that. We've been on the go since we got back to the States. Not all of us have time to lounge around in fur when there's nothing else going on."

"And there's the basis of his problem." Mark turned back to me. "We need to get your wolf out tonight, Lucas. Since it's scared and hiding now, we're going to have to do this the hard way, and in a way that's not going to damage it farther." He let out a heavy sigh. "I won't have a damaged wolf in my territory, it's too dangerous. I don't want to put you down."

The way he said it, I had no doubt he would do just that.

Vash stood and glared at him with her hands on her hips. "You will not hurt Lucas. I won't allow it." Sparks flew from her hair, dancing around her in a vortex of power.

I grabbed her hand. "He doesn't want to, Vash. We're all going to be okay."

"It's amazing the things I miss when traffic makes me late." A woman walked into the room. She radiated power like Harris or Garnet did.

"Persephone, you have impeccable timing." Mark seemed to relax a little more as the woman came over to him.

"I try." She looked around the room. Her azure gaze lingered on me for a moment but was drawn to Vash. "What are you, my dear? I can't say as I've ever met one of your kind."

"We're not worried about Vash right now." Mark stepped between the two. "Sergeant Lucas is our problem. Maybe with your magic and mine working together, we can bring his wolf out safely. I don't know how much damage it will do to him if we don't do this."

Briar huffed again. "I have to agree. I've never heard of a wolf not shifting on the night of their first full moon."

"Nor have I." Mark looked at Vash. "Now, young lady, if you'll let us work with your master without your interference, we'll set things as right as we can." He sighed heavily. "Can't say as we'll be able to fix the PTSD triggered by howls. You may be a lone wolf forever."

I was okay with that. Since leaving the service, I wasn't sure I wanted to bend my knee to anyone on a regular basis again. "We'll work through that."

"Yes, we will." Mark nodded curtly, and then looked at Vash. "Please let us do what we can."

Vash pursed her lips. "Those of fur are different from the rest of us, even those of us of smoke. Yes. Please make him all right." She became smoke for a moment, then solidified on the back on the couch. "I will stay *here*, to ensure he's safe."

It didn't cease to amaze me how her speech was so often counter to her apparent age. In a lot of ways that disappearance made it all the more important that I be there to help her in this new different world.

Persephone's eyes grew wide. "A genie? You're a genie. I have to talk with you when this is all over."

"We need to focus, Persephone." Mark waved his hand slightly like he was trying to get her attention. "Briar, you know Vash better than I do."

Briar nodded but didn't say anything.

"Good." Mark looked at me. "Sergeant Lucas. It's time."

"What do I need to do?" For the first time since I woke up, I was aware of my nudity on the couch. I wished there was a blanket or something I could cover myself with.

"Just lay there and don't fight when your wolf comes out. Persephone and I will coax it out. You'll be aware of everything we do, and you'll feel your wolf when he comes out. We'll do what we can to make sure the two of you bond. That will make it easier."

I just nodded and braced myself for what was to come next.

21

"Sergeant Lucas, I need you to relax." The sound of Persephone's voice surrounded me. I heard it through my ears but it hit me deeper like she was inside my head. "Don't fight, if you fight, this is going to be more painful than it has to be."

"I'm trying." I took a deep breath and did my best to push my fears and worries aside. It was hard. Letting other people have control wasn't something I was used to.

"Take deep breaths." Persephone's presence around me dove deeper. "With each one, forget everything but my voice. Focus on me and only me."

Doing as she instructed, I started to feel light and insubstantial. I wondered if this was what Vash felt like when she became smoke.

Somewhere nearby, her child's laughter made me feel even lighter.

"That's right. Ease into this." Persephone's voice was even, almost like a soft spring breeze.

"Come to me." Mark's presence was heavier, earthier than Persephone's, but it wasn't meant for me, it was calling to the wolf hiding deep inside me.

From a dark corner of my mind, or my body, I couldn't really tell which, the wolf unwound from the tight scared ball of fur it had retreated into when I freaked out at the howls. Its whine escaped my lips. A feeling of being beaten and scared filled me. Everything tightened.

"Stay relaxed." Persephone pushed her gentle energy into me, forcing more cool relaxing breezes to swirl around me.

The wolf circled, uncertain, deep within me. It wanted to return to the safe ball of fur where nothing could hurt it.

I understood. I didn't want to hear howling ever again. The howling might endanger Vash. The howling had destroyed my unit. The howling had wrecked my life.

"No, come to me." Mark's voice held more command than it had previously.

"It's okay." Vash filled me with her light, pushing it through the darkness until I could see the wolf inside me.

I'd never seen him before. Everything had just been feelings and vague sensations. He was bigger than I'd expected, easily the size of a large pony. The way he kept his head and gaze down reminded me of a beaten dog my unit had come across in the desert. It had had open cuts on its back and head. The thing had been a large, powerful dog at one point in its life, but due to abuse, it had been reduced to a quivering shade of its former self. It had died the night we found it. The damage had been too great, and it hadn't wanted to go on even though we would've fed it and given it the best life possible. I didn't want that for the wolf inside me.

Kneeling, I reached a hand out to him. "It's okay. I'm sorry I scared you before."

He looked at me but didn't stare at my face. He stopped walking in tight circles and stood there shaking.

"Come, feel the world." Mark continued his own urging, like he could feel the wolf responding to me. "You deserve to run free."

The way my wolf shook, he wasn't sure what he wanted to do.

"You are a very pretty wolf." Vash stood there in my mental plain next to me. She was more of a shape in red smoke and sparks than a little girl. "Come on. Maybe we can play. Would you like that?"

Where he would not meet my gaze, he stared at Vash.

I held out my hand to him. "She's right, you are a handsome wolf."

He took a step toward me, came clear of the shadows, and became even more solid. He gleamed silver. I'd never seen an animal of exactly that color before. He was magical and powerful, just like Vash. The other wolves I'd seen at Mark's cabin hadn't felt as magical as mine did. I couldn't tell if that was because we were inside my mind, or if he really was different.

"That's right, come to us." Mark's voice interrupted my thoughts, but not in a jarring way.

"I've never seen your like," Persephone said. "So exotic."

The wolf stopped and glanced around. He raised his nose and sniffed.

Vash took a couple of steps closer to him, becoming more solid as she did. "Lucas is my guardian. That means you will be, too." She touched his ear.

If a wolf could truly smile, he would've. A simple feeling of joy and happiness flowed off him as she moved her hand down his head.

For the first time, he looked up and met my gaze. His eyes were as silver as the rest of him. As we stared at each other, they seemed to glow until they engulfed me.

"Good. Come on, let go," Mark's voice was louder as the wolf took the final steps.

My hands shook as I reached for the wolf and buried my fingers in his silver fur. He was softer than I had expected. The other wolves had a slightly rough edge to them, but not him.

Then he stepped into me.

The silver light flooded through me. Pain seared through every bone in my body. Together the wolf and I yelped and screamed.

"Don't fight it." Mark's voice held more command than it had. But that command helped me relax and the pain receded.

I was still on my back, and it didn't feel right. Rolling off the couch, I landed on four legs. The world's strange colors and many scents hit me all at the same time. The breeze coming through the open porch door ruffled my fur. I wanted to run. No, not me, the wolf, but we'd become one.

Our first step was awkward, stumbling slightly until I understood I needed to let the wolf control this body. Again, I was having to let go and not be in total control.

We turned toward the open, it promised freedom more than the house with its strange smells.

I did my best to let the wolf have control over our actions.

Two wolves were at our side, both dark and dangerous, but we were nearly as large as they were.

"Let's run." Mark's voice came from the black wolf on my left; I could only assume the other wolf was Briar.

I'd never seen his wolf form before. It seemed to fit his human form more than Mark's wolf form did his.

Running came naturally as our paws hit the grass. The trappings of humanity fell away a few feet from the house. The back porch ended and the wilds began.

With the two alphas at our side, we ran across the hillside, wanting to lose ourselves in the woods. The forest seemed to be holding its breath like all the animals there knew it was a night of predators. But there was more. The scent of smoke.

We stopped and turned.

"What's wrong?" Mark stopped and glanced around.

"Smoke." We couldn't pinpoint a location for it.

Farther up the hill, a wolf howled. The sound shook me. Forgetting the smoke, I shoved my wolf aside and turned away from the howl as more answered it. The first couple of steps were awkward, then the wolf slipped back in control so that we could run from the howling.

"Wait, there's nothing to be afraid of." Mark ran after us.

Briar raced at his side. "Sergeant Lucas, stop."

It was easy enough to block them out. The howling pushed us onward.

The forest fell away as our paws hit pavement.

Tires squealed, momentarily blocking out the howls.

A horn blared but we kept running and soon the forest engulfed us again.

"Lucas." Vash's voice was a mix of soothing breeze and soft bells. "It's okay. The howls aren't going to get you."

She appeared in the trees only a few feet from us. The sparks from her hair lit up the night.

We tried to stop. Neither of us wanted to hurt Vash. Turning away, we hit a tree hard.

Vash touched our ear. "Oh, Lucas. You'll be okay."

The scent of smoke hit us again. I recognized it. "Vash, shield. They're here." But the words came out as yips and whines.

She straightened and glanced around, like she'd understood what I'd tried to tell her.

"I won't let them hurt you." She wrapped her arms around our neck and her sparks cascaded around us.

We expected her to teleport us out of there, but the forest seemed to come to her defense. Leaves and pine needles from the forest floor swirled around us until they formed a dome of loamy death. Vines and briars moved through it until there was nothing of us escaping for the effrits to sense.

"Stay quiet." Vash buried her face in our ruff. "They won't search long. I should've been more careful with my magic."

We couldn't offer her comfort beyond bending our neck around so we put our muzzle on her back and blew a breath through her hair that wasn't sparking as much as it had been earlier.

The smell of smoke and embers grew strong enough to permeate our protected area. The effrits were right on top of us. Would Vash's magic and our new fangs and claws be enough to save us or would our fight end there on the side of a mountain west of Denver?

"You aren't welcome here!" Mark's voice filled the night. It hadn't come through my head, but my ears.

"This doesn't concern you, wolf, go back to your hunt and leave us to ours." The voice was rough and heavily accented. It reminded me of a man I had met in the souk one time who sat on a small stool with a hookah on the table behind him. It was the ultimate smoker's voice.

"You're trespassing," Mark countered.

"And you've lied to us." The effrit snarled and the fur along our spine stood up.

My wolf wanted to explode from our tiny sanctuary and attack it, but I held him back. Even with Mark and Briar there, the odds were we couldn't take it without more magic than we had access to.

"How?" Mark snapped. "It doesn't matter. The moon is full and my temper is short. Leave! You can bring your grievance to me in my city home tomorrow. If you don't leave, I *will* have my wolves tear you apart."

The rest of the pack slipped out of the forest around us. Their scent was comforting. For the first time, I wanted the wolves near me.

"Do you think you'd be the first wolves to fall to us?" The effrit didn't sound like he was ready to back down.

"That's why we brought our witches," Briar spoke for the first time.

"Unless you want to see how much damage we can do to you and this hillside, back off." Persephone sounded pissed.

"The mongrel is one of ours and if you continue to hide her, you will suffer her fate."

I really hoped Urson was going to be fast getting the magical weapons ready, I was ready to stop the effrits once and for all.

The smell of smoke faded leaving only the scent of the pack around us.

Vash relaxed and straightened. "Thanks." Her whisper sent shivers across oury fur as the protective dome fell away.

Mark and Briar stood there, fully clothed. Persephone, Cin Kilkari, and Agent May also stood there with the pack of wolves scattered around us.

It was like popping out of a hole with a unit of Army Rangers with large firearms pointed in my direction. I wished I could hold up my hands and surrender, but my wolf understood and dropped us to the ground and rolled over in submission.

"Enough." Mark snapped, sounding like his patience for the evening was done. "Everyone back to the house." He stared at Vash. "I don't want those effrits sensing you on my land again."

She knelt at our side and looked up at him. "Yes, sir."

We wanted to snap at him for making her cower, but he was the alpha, and not to be questioned.

"Good." His human form blurred and again his massive black wolf stood there for a second before running off. The rest of the pack followed him. The way they all stayed silent sent an eerie chill through me. It didn't feel natural, but I was thankful they stayed silent.

"Come on, you two." Cin held out her hand to Vash. "Let's get back to the cabin."

Questions were forming in my head as we got to our feet and followed them back through the forest. The night hadn't gone nearly as I had expected it to, and with the moon just reaching its apex above us, it wasn't even close to done.

16

The room at Garnet's house looked the same, but that was all. Everything felt different, smelled different. Two days after the full moon and I was still trying to sort out what was happening. Briar and Kilkari told me it was just my wolf blending over to my human side, augmenting everything, but it was so different. There was a small draft coming through a cracked window that I hadn't noticed before. Every time she opened the fridge, I had the urge to run into the kitchen, grab the bowl of rotting salad that was in the back on the bottom shelf, and take it out to the dumpster, but that would involve enduring the reek of the dumpster. I'd done that the day before and wasn't looking forward to doing that again any time soon. How people could endure the fowl reek was beyond me.

"You're awake." Vash came into the room without knocking. Her voice sounded louder than it had before the full moon.

Everyone kept telling me the enhanced senses, even in human form, were a big advantage to being a werewolf. They also assured me it wasn't uncommon to have a bit of adjustment time to get used to things. I had hoped to have time to adjust. I didn't want to remain a virtual prisoner in Garnet's home until we found a way to defeat the effrit, or they just gave up and went away. If they were anything like the mortal terrorists I was used to dealing with, they weren't going to give up until they were either dead or imprisoned.

"Yeah, I'm awake. What's going on today?" I grabbed a shirt out of my duffle and pulled it on. We'd just bought it a few days earlier and it was already too tight. My body had taken to being a werewolf better than anyone Briar or Mark had ever seen. Even Kilkari, who said he put on a bit of muscle, hadn't merged his wolf's mass with his human to the extent that I had. I didn't look forward to buying new clothes again. The most shocking thing, at least to me, was the change in my hair. Every hair on my body was now silver, matching my wolf's fur.

"Briar just got a call from the bear in Denver, said you would be there in a little while. Can I go? I'm tired of waiting." Vash frowned. "Even the games Garnet plays with me are getting boring. The magic in them isn't real."

Garnet had introduced Vash to video games. It kept the two of them occupied, but it wasn't fooling Vash. After a couple of days, she had mastered the games and was ready for something more complex. I could appreciate that. The kid was smart, maybe too smart considering how powerful she was. It was going to make keeping her safe a lot harder.

"I don't think I want Urson meeting you." I sat on the bed and pulled on my boots. "He knows about you, but knowing about you isn't the same as meeting you. Vash, I'm still figuring out who I can trust. I've had to trust Briar, Kilkari, and Mark. There's something that makes me think we can trust Urson, but I'm not totally sure. He wanted me to bring you, something about you adding to his spell, but I'd rather keep you safe here."

"That's smart." Briar appeared in the doorway. The scent of wolf preceded him by mere seconds. "But I'm pretty sure Urson's one of the good guys."

"I'll draw my own conclusions." I shook my legs to knock any wrinkles out of my jeans. After years of sleeping, ready for combat at a moment's notice, I normally slept partially clothed so I could roll out and go.

"That a good attitude to have." Briar leaned against the doorframe. "Honestly, after Vash adapts to our world, I might just get the two of you working for me."

I stared at him and shook my head. "I don't think I'd be good at enforcement. I'm done following orders."

Briar nodded. "I get that. But you know, we're going to have to get you a job, unless you're independently wealthy. And I know that isn't the truth."

"I figure I'll work on that once we get the effrits taken care of." I hoped Urson's weapons were going to be able to handle the effrits so we could get started on our new lives.

"Got my fingers crossed that will be soon." Briar stepped out of the way so I could exit the room. "May and I are getting tired of babysitting the two of you."

I grinned at him. "And you're doing a great job of it."

"Now, let's get up to Denver and pick up the arms so we can work out a plan to take the effrits." Briar let me walk in front of him as we walked down the hall.

The front door opened and Harris walked in carrying a couple of boxes. "Looks like you're ready for donuts."

Stopping, I stared at him for a moment. "How did you know I was ready for breakfast?"

Harris shrugged. "I'm a good mage. Things tend to go my way."

"Magic is good for that." Vash hurried along at my side. "Sometimes luck is stronger even than wishes."

"And I'm happy about that, since I can't do wishes." Harris opened a box and held it out to us. "Since I didn't know what anyone liked, I got an assortment."

"Maple is good." I reached in and took one covered in light brown frosting. "Vash, the ones with sprinkles are good too."

Harris held the box a little lower so Vash could reach it.

Vash's face wrinkled in concentration. "What are sprinkles?"

"They're the multicolored dots on top of the donuts." I pointed to one in the box. "That one."

Vash picked it up. "It's a pastry."

I nodded. "Exactly. They come with lots of different flavors on them." The maple flavor flooded across my taste buds with so much intensity that it made me wonder what it would taste like to lick a bleeding maple tree. If I was honest about it, the flavor was nearly too sweet, but I didn't care.

When Vash bit into hers, a grin spread across her delicate features. "This is good." She looked at Harris. "Thank you, Gavin, for bringing donuts."

"You're welcome, Vash." Harris gave her a slight bow.

Vash giggled. "No one bows to a djinn, we bow to mortals, that's one of the rules. But thank you, Gavin."

Someone knocked on the front door.

Gavin handed the donuts to me. "I'll get it."

"Thanks, Gavin," Garnet shouted from the kitchen.

I turned and put the box of donuts on the dining room table, then grabbed a second one, a vanilla one.

"You look like you're going somewhere," Marzie Campbell's voice came from the door.

Smacking my head, I groaned. "We're supposed to look at houses today."

Marzie stepped into the living room carrying a tray of coffees. "Bad timing? Or did you just forget? Wasn't sure how many to grab."

"Both." I finished off the second donut. "We've got to see a bear in Denver." I wasn't used to forgetting things or having a screwed-up schedule. We needed the weapons, but Vash and I needed a home too.

"Well then—" Marzie shrugged and set down the coffees "—I guess it's a good thing I found us some places to look at between the Springs and Denver, and scheduled us a little bit of time between showings. Let's go and do everything."

Vash looked between me and Marzie. "Wait, she gets to go and I don't?"

With a sigh, I lowered myself to my knee and looked her in the eyes. "Vash. There aren't effrits looking for Marzie. We're trying to keep you safe."

She opened her mouth as if to object. I put a finger on her tiny lips.

"Vash, I know that you can shield yourself from the effrits, but we don't know who all they have talked to, except that they have spoken to the Denver wolves and we trust them. They may or may not have talked to the bears. Until we can be sure we can trust them, I don't want them to see you, or get your scent. Please, stay here. I won't command you, but I will ask you." If I understood the way my being the holder of her bell worked, I could order her to do my bidding, but that wasn't who I was. I couldn't bring myself to usurp her free will.

She looked down, submissively. "I will stay, Lucas."

Garnet came out of the kitchen and put a hand on Vash's shoulder. "We'll have fun today. Maybe we'll go and find Lucas some new shirts. I've seen what he likes, maybe we can get something that will set off his new hair."

I looked up at Garnet and smiled. "Thank you, but you don't have to do that. I can do it, maybe tonight we can go out and get some dinner and do some shopping." It would be similar to twisting a knife in my gut, but I'd endure it.

"Okay then." Garnet took Vash's hand. "We'll hold him to that, won't we?"

Vash looked a little confused between us. "I'd like that."

Her shifting from little girl to sounding more like an adult amazed me. It made me wonder if she felt as confused as it could make me. Sometimes I wondered if more of the supernatural beings were like her and less like humans. It was true that most of the ones I'd met were things like witches and shifters, but some of them spoke of things like fae. If I ever met them, would those be like humans, or fluid in their actions like Vash?

"Good, sounds like a plan." I looked up at Marzie. "Guess we can get going."

"If you don't mind sitting in the car while we deal with the bears in Denver." Briar headed toward the front door.

"Sure." Marzie pulled up one of the cups of coffee. "I'll have my computer with me. Lots to do. Actually, if you don't mind driving, I can get a lot more done today than I'd planned. Got some things to order for the latest house flip."

"Sure, we've got room." Briar opened the door and headed out onto the porch. "Our day just gets busier and busier."

I followed him as Gavin and Marzie hurried after us. With everything going on, I was ready for life to slow down so Vash and I could sort things out and settle into Colorado. But that wasn't going to happen, not until I knew for sure that Vash was safe.

17

I wasn't sure what was more frustrating, looking at houses that didn't fit our needs or battling Denver traffic. It was a fairly busy day on the roads and we ended up running a bit later reaching Urson's workshop than we'd planned.

Briar parked where we'd parked before. The gate was again open. There didn't seem to be as many people around.

Before we cleared the gate, Briar stopped and sniffed. "They're not as aggressive when it isn't the full moon."

Harris chuckled. "Or maybe they aren't as upset with just two wolves visiting them."

"They've also taken our measure," I added. In most of my dealings with informants and their like, I'd always found the second meeting was easier than the first. "It'll be hard to surprise them."

"And you do realize that bears have better hearing than wolves." Urson appeared in the tall wide door of his workshop. He wore a light blue T-shirt that was so tight that I wondered how he'd managed to get it on. Overall, he was cleaner, less scruffy than he had been, and I wondered if it was due to the passing of the moon, or if he was done working for the day and ready for something that didn't involve forges and hammers.

"I've been told a few times." Briar stopped a few feet from the door.

"Then maybe one of these days you'll remember." Urson stepped out of our path and waved us into the workshop. "And maybe one of these days you'll learn to be on time and respect other people's time as you do your own." He glanced behind us and frowned. "And maybe, one day wolves can remember instructions."

For a second, I wondered what he meant, then remembered. "Vash. I'm sorry, Digger, I forgot. Too much going on." I didn't want him to realize that I didn't totally trust him, particularly when it came to Vash. Even if he'd asked for her presence, we could work out something without it.

Briar didn't respond to the jibe or my words to Urson. "So, let's see the weapons you've made for us. I understand that you've already sent your bill and it's been paid."

"That's correct. I just received confirmation of the payment. It is nice doing business with you." With a wave to me that cut off any more apology, Urson strode over to his workbench where two Pelican cases lay. "Let's start with the easier of the two, the one that will see the most use." He opened the smaller one. Inside the foam cutouts, a handgun that was slightly larger than a Glock lay. There were a couple of boxes of ammo across the top of the case. Urson pulled out the gun and presented it to me with open hands.

It didn't make any sense that the firearm had

been easier to create than a sword, but then I didn't know as much about swords. I lifted it gently from him. My first thought was that it was heavier than I'd expected. The metal of the barrel was darker than any barrel I'd seen. It wasn't crafted of steel. When I pointed it toward the wall, the fit of the handle was perfect. My hands were large enough that most guns felt small, but this one didn't. There was a tingle that was beginning to feel familiar—magic.

"I think he likes it," Harris said.

"You think?" Briar added.

"What?" I lowered the gun and looked at them.

"You're smiling like a kid at Christmas." Harris laughed. "I take it you did good, Urson."

Urson blew out a loud huff. "Of course, I did good. I don't get complaints on my work, but he is a happy wolf."

I shrugged and put the gun back in the case before they said anything more. "What's not to be happy about? It's a gorgeous piece of work."

"Yes, it is." Urson pulled it free of the foam again. He popped out the magazine. "It holds thirteen bullets. An odd number, I know, but you'll find that magic often works better in odd numbers. You can get nine millimeters off the shelf, or come back and tell me what you need and I'll fill your order. I have a lot of options, depending on what kind of trouble you're expecting." He slid the cartridge home again and it snapped in place with a satisfying snap before he returned it to its case.

Then he pulled out the ammo cases. "Since you're still learning a bit about magic, I color-coded them." He tipped the cases and spilled large, powerful bullets into his huge hands. "The bluish ones are ice projectiles. Finding information on the effrits is difficult, but I assure you, hit one of them with these and you'll make an impact. I don't know how much help the reddish ones will be, but they're fireballs. After they strike your target, they'll explode. Against a creature of smoke and flames it might not do any lasting damage, but I bet you'll stop any magic it's using, and distract it while it pulls itself back together. Since I was working on a tight schedule, I couldn't do as many of the yellow ones as I'd have liked, but they call lightning as they pass through the air." He picked up one of the yellow bullets and held it up to the light. "I thought you might like having them. If you want more, I'll have them next month."

I stared at the bullets, intrigued by the way the light danced off the yellow one. "How did you color-code them without screwing up the metal or the firing?"

"Magic. There's a lot magic can do when you're good at it, and my witch and I are. Actually, he's a druid." Faster than any human could dream of moving, he got the bullets back in the case. "Which brings me to one last thing." He put the ammo back in the case and pulled a leather holster and belt from the spot it had occupied in the case top. "I know we have open carry here in Colorado, but sometimes you'll want to be a little more subtle than others. As long as the gun and holster are together, humans won't be able to see it, well, non-magical humans that is."

Harris cocked his head. "More druid magic?"

"You have a druid near you, Gavin, perhaps you should go talk to him." Urson handed me the holster. "Put it on."

I slipped it around my waist and the belt holes weren't at the right places to tighten. When I got back to Garnet's I'd need to break out an ice pick and make a new hole.

Urson frowned. "You changed with your first moon. More than just your hair." He held out his hand for the belt. "I will have that fixed in a moment. It is good that you and your wolf have found common ground. I heard it wasn't an easy moon for you."

Handing the belt and holster to him, I glanced at Briar.

"The shifter community isn't that large." Briar held up his hands in an empty gesture.

"One of my bears is the husband to one of the pack wolves." Urson took a leather punch from a drawer and took a moment to make a new hole before handing the belt back to me. "It is hard that the howls undo you. I have sent a message to Mark that if you need a teacher who doesn't howl, I'll be happy to see you through your first year or so."

The belt fit perfectly, but I stopped as I slipped the tongue through my belt straps and stared from Urson to Briar. "Year or so? How long does it take to get used to?" I'd figured that after a few moons I'd be safe to be around and have everything sorted out.

"Wolves aren't meant to be alone," Briar used the same words Mark had used when we'd talked about what had happened during the moon. At that time, Mark thought it might be a good idea if Kilkari was to join me during the next few moons. He'd apparently made great strides in getting over eating the sheriff. "Sure, we're making arrangements to not get your PTSD flaring, but if something goes wrong, we might have to come up with alternatives. Urson and his bears might be an answer. Bears don't howl."

"And as long as you can handle your mead, we have very festive full moons around here." Urson handed me the gun again. "I'm pretty sure of who you are, David, you'd be welcome."

"Thanks." It was the only thing I could think of to say and it was for more than just the offer of a place to shift. As I slid the gun into the holster, the whole thing tingled and I suddenly felt whole. I ran my fingers along the grip. It was at the perfect height for a quick draw.

Urson chuckled. "Your smile is enough thanks. One last thing before we move on. All great weapons have to have names. You're a warrior, you know this."

Although I'd never named one of my own, I understood. There'd been several men in my unit who'd named their weapons. "Yes, you named it?"

"I did." Urson waved to where the gun hung on my side. "She is Stormbringer. I think you'll enjoy her roar of thunder."

With a soft sigh, I slipped my hand around her wooden grip. Stormbringer. A gun that could shoot bullets of lightning. I liked it. "Thank you, Digger."

He reached for the larger case and slid it across the workbench. "Now for the easy one." He flipped open the case. A long sword lay there. It was made with the same dark metal as Stormbringer's barrel. There was more to it, and it seemed to draw in the light.

"We got lucky and my druid was able to finish some of the spells Agent May and Harris found that can be used to bind a djinn." Urson lifted the sword, pulled it free of the simple leather scabbard and the room dimmed slightly. "Run an effrit through with this and it will be bound to the blade and completely under your control." He handed me the blade, hilt first. The position was ceremonial and it would've been simple for me to run him through with his own craftsmanship. That was why people skilled in swordsmanship passed swords to each other in such a way. It was a sign of trust.

My hand shook slightly as I reached for it. I'd held a few swords over time, but it wasn't a weapon I was familiar with. Like Stormbringer, it was heavier than I expected. The point dipped slightly before I adjusted my grip on the pommel.

"It's a good thing your arms and legs stayed the same length after your shift, or the blade would be too short." Urson leaned against the workbench.

"Too short?" I swished the sword through the air. It felt awkward even if it was made for me. I was going to need to practice with it for a while.

"I am sure you are not used to hearing that, but yes." Urson grinned. "A sword is made for the arm and hand of a particular person, or it's awkward. In the old days, we even crafted training swords to match the youth who would be using it. They never used a practice sword for more than a year or so before they'd outgrown it and the sword was recast. Often we even used the same metal so the spirit of the blade grew with the man or woman using it."

"Spirit of the blade?" My forearms complained about the swings. "You said this blade is for catching effrit. Does it have a spirit?"

Urson returned the sword to its scabbard. "Not yet. A sword gains its spirit from the first thing it kills. That is also when the sword will gain its name. There are no special magical words that will let you entrap the effrits, nor have we added any other magics to it yet, there wasn't time. Should you decide you wish to expand upon what the sword can do, we'll sit down and discuss it. Maybe your djinn could help with that at that time. "

He made it sound like we were getting a better off-road package for a Jeep. I was still learning about magic, but somehow, I thought it might be harder than that. Vash might know more about that than I did.

"I'll keep that in mind." I ran my hand over the smooth leather scabbard laying in the case. It might be a good idea to learn to use it, but the gun was more along the lines I was used to.

"Good." Urson closed the case after I pulled my hand back. "I am happy that you're pleased with the weapons. If I can help you again in the future, please, let me know. And I mean that in anything, not just weapons. Now, I have an appointment to keep and unlike some people, I don't like being late."

"Thank you, Urson." Briar nodded then headed toward the door.

"I'll check back with you on that commission we talked about a couple of weeks ago." Harris paused before turning.

"The stars are almost aligned for that casting. I'll let you know when we're ready." Urson pointed to the door. "Now let's get everyone moving. I have places to be."

"Thanks, Digger." I took the two cases from the worktable. Even through the case, the sword's magic hummed through me. I felt better having the gear we were going to need to bring down the effrits and keep Vash safe. It made dealing with Denver traffic worth the hassle.

18

"Turn here," Marzie instructed Briar as he headed toward the last house on her list. She'd adjusted the last two showings after we'd gotten stuck in traffic on the loop while leaving Urson's workshop.

If I was going to be honest with her, I didn't feel like I was being overly picky, but I did want something I could consider defensible, and that still had room for Vash and me. We might not have a lot at that moment, but somehow, I figured she was going to acquire things quickly. At least, most of the little girls I'd ever heard about tended to do that. I wanted her to have plenty of closet space. All I really needed was a couple of drawers to fold clothes into, a bed, and a gun shop. Stormbringer wasn't going to be my only firearm and having a spot, even a corner in a bedroom, where I could clean and keep firearms in good repair was going to be a plus. But I hadn't mentioned that to Marzie, figuring she didn't need to know about that if I didn't want her to.

"Right here." Marzie pointed at the drive that was at the end of the road near the top of a hill.

There were a fair number of trees around the place, but a nice pasture rolled away from the house along the west side.

We bounced a couple of times along several ruts that made it look like the drive had washed out from time to time. With a proper truck or SUV, it wouldn't be a huge problem.

Briar swore a couple of times and white-knuckled the wheel. "I hope they'll take off a bit for drive repair."

"Hard to tell." Marzie closed her laptop and leaned over the seat. "Looks like a car up there." She pointed toward the big Dodge SUV parked in front of a log cabin.

The place wasn't as big as Mark's pack lodge, but it looked a lot homier, at least to me. It reminded me of one of the older cabins back on the family ranch. My folks had made extra money off the place renting it out to hunters in the fall and winter.

As we got out of the car, Marzie looked around. "A little smaller than I expected. The listing's for two thousand square feet."

A tall man slipped out of the SUV and took a couple of steps toward us. "Ms. Campbell?"

"Mr. Watabe?" Marzie headed right up to him and thrust out her hand. "Thanks for meeting us with such a short change of schedule."

"No problem. I had another showing that I could move up." After he released her hand, he looked at the three of us standing behind her. "Which of you would be the prospective buyer?" He sounded a little nervous.

I raised my hand. "That would be me."

Marzie turned. "Mr. Watabe, this is retired

Sergeant Lucas.”

Even though I wasn't sure it was necessary, Marzie had insisted on introducing me that way. She said that since Colorado Springs had such a large military presence, it helped open doors and might even help us get better prices on things.

Watabe shook my hand. “Sergeant Lucas, I hope this house will work for you. I know it's a little out of the way, but it's on fifty acres, and the nearest neighbors are nearly a quarter-mile away due to their pastures. The other land around here is still large ranches, so as long as you keep the fences up, not much to bother you.”

I nodded. “Nice to know.”

“Is it just going to be you?” He cast a glance back and Briar and Harris who were leaning on the car.

“Me and my daughter.” It felt strange claiming Vash as mine, but that needed to get easier. I was her guardian, her protector. She was going to be with me for a long time, unless the effrits got the better of us.

“Ah, children are wonderful. I've got three of my own.” He turned toward the door. “How old is yours?”

That was one of those questions we'd been debating how to answer. Everyone felt like most people would by her visual age. “Eight. Her mother died years ago.”

“Single dad; that can be rough.” He opened the door. “I don't know how I'd handle it if something happened to my wife and left me with the boys.”

“We all adjust,” Marzie said, stepping between me and Watabe. “We'll take a look around.”

"Oh, sure." Watabe held the door open.

The front room was fairly large with hardwood floors and bay windows that looked out onto the rolling pasture beyond. I could see to the foothills a couple of miles away. Even Pikes Peak was visible. I nodded, liking what I saw. Sure, it would be smaller with furniture, but I wasn't expecting to have tons of people over for parties and such.

We headed toward the kitchen when Marzie froze and started looking around like a scared rabbit.

"What's wrong?" All I could see was a recently updated kitchen with marble countertops and stainless-steel appliances.

"A ghost." Marzie's response came out the barest whisper.

My hand reflexively moved to my hip, Stormbringer was hanging there, unfired, but it made me feel safer. "Where?"

Marzie pursed her lips and skittered her glance around the room. "Not totally sure. Like the whole kitchen."

"Are you a medium or a witch?" I couldn't help myself; I kept my hand near Stormbringer. Thing was, I didn't think Watabe would like it if I shot up the house before even putting a bid in on it.

"Yes. More of a medium." Marzie shook her head. "I don't know where it is exactly. Not sure you want a place with a ghost, but Cin and I might be able to get rid of it for you. Or you could ask Gavin to do it."

"We'll see." I huffed but didn't relax. "I like the place so far."

"Other than the ghost, I do too." Marzie squared her shoulder, gave her long black hair a shake, and continued through the kitchen.

"How big a problem would that be, if we don't find a way to make it…" I tried to remember what one of the guys in the unit used to call it. He'd been big into superstitious stuff. He'd have probably had an easier time adjusting to my new life than I was having. "Move on. Is that the right term?"

"It is." Marzie opened the door to one of the bedrooms. "Depends. Cin and Chad have her mother still around, not that they've tried, beyond asking politely, to get her to move on. She's still part of the family. She and Chad don't always get along, and the fact that he can't see or sense her only makes things worse."

"I bet Vash can see ghosts." It made sense that a djinn who was able to turn into smoke could see ghosts.

Marzie stayed at the door as I went into the room. "Yeah, probably."

The room was smaller than some of the bedrooms we'd looked at earlier in the day but larger than the one I'd had growing up. It might make a good place for Vash, even had a small walk-in closet. "Not bad. Doesn't look to have its own bathroom."

"Does Vash even need one?" Marzie dropped her voice to a mere whisper.

Heading out of the room, I shrugged. "That might be a better question for Garnet or Cin. Can't say as I know the answer to that one. She's been eating and drinking. All that mass has to go somewhere."

Opening the next door, Marzie nodded. "Unless she turns it all into magic. She'll need energy from somewhere."

Something else I hadn't stopped to think about. I'd met several people who used magic but hadn't stopped to ask where it came from. From what Urson had said when talking about crafting Stormbringer and the sword, there were different types of magic. I wondered if I would get a chance to sit down and talk to Harris or Garnet about it sometime soon. The more I understood, the better I'd be able to survive the new world I found myself in.

The master bedroom was nearly twice the size of the bedroom across the hall. There were windows looking out on the pasture and foothills as well as one with a view of the trees a safe distance out the south side of the house. The walk-in closet was also larger than the other room, and the master bath. It made me smile. There wasn't a soft feminine side to it that had been prominent in the other houses. The garden tub had thick rocky tiles around the base and smooth chocolate tiles around the top. The granite sink base was a little higher than normal and done in dark stone. The shower was mostly glass but lined in the dark stone-like tiles that were around the tub.

"I wouldn't have to remodel this." I put my hands on the counter and only had to bend slightly. The image in the mirror was only slightly what I remembered. Not an ounce of fat was on my cheeks and I couldn't tell if that plus the silver hair made me look older, or simply distinguished.

"No, this looks like it's in good shape. Very

manly too." Marzie stood in the doorway between the bathroom and bedroom. "Honestly, normally I'd recommend having a homeowner redo this to something that would appeal to the wife more, but this is very you."

"Good." I turned from the image I was still getting used to. "Let's look at the bathroom Vash will use. Even if she doesn't need a toilet, a young girl needs a place to learn makeup and such."

Marzie laughed as she turned. "I can see you calling Cin or Garnet for help with that."

"Probably." I followed as we left the bedroom and went down the hall to the last two doors.

"I'm sure they'll be happy to help. Cin's got major empty-nest syndrome since their girls have both headed off to college. I don't know about Garnet. I can help too, mine would be from remembering how I learned since I have a son, not a daughter."

"I'll keep that in mind." The hall bath was a basic normal bath. Everything was at normal height and a neutral beige that could be for either a boy or a girl. Looking at the walls, I wondered how Vash would want to decorate it.

The final door led to a set of stairs dropping down into a basement. I went first, turning on the lights as I went. The basement was finished, but still a single large room. There was a set of cabinets along one wall with a couple of small windows set high along the ceiling. It had a short thick carpet that was still in good shape.

"Almost a blank slate down here." Marzie looked around.

I nodded. "Yeah, it is." There was a lot I could do with the space. It wasn't long enough for an indoor shooting range, but it was close. I definitely had room for a gun bench. Hell, I could even set up a reloading station. That was, if I could talk Urson out of some of his secrets and Vash could replicate the magic. "Okay, I want to try for it."

"There's a couple of outbuildings we could look at." Marzie turned back toward the stairs.

I started to shake my head, then stopped. "If we do that then I won't seem too eager, right?"

Marzie smiled. "And you're smart too. Yes." She pulled out her phone as we walked up the stairs. "According to the listing, it's been on the market nine months. That's odd for the location, although it is a little farther out than a lot of people like."

"What are the chances the ghost is making people uncomfortable?" I turned out the lights as we reached the top of the stairs.

"Good thought." She turned and pointed at me. "A lot of people can sense more than they understand. She could be making people skittish and skittish people don't tend to buy houses."

I huffed. "If she turns out to be a problem, we'll deal with her."

Marzie paused in the living room and looked toward the front door. "Mr. Watabe, we're heading into the backyard. Is it okay to use this door?"

The seller's agent hurried across the room. "Of course. Here, let me get this for you."

"Thanks." Marzie gave him a warm smile as we walked past him and through the rugged French doors.

Two outbuildings sat a short distance from the cabin. The trees encroached on them but weren't thick enough to be a problem as far as keeping the place safe.

"Looks like someone has had horses here in the past." Marzie pointed toward the smaller of the buildings which was a lean-to, open to the south.

"That would be nice but not sure if it's going to work out for us." I walked toward the other building that looked more like a storage building.

"Something to ask around about if you really want a horse or something." Marzie followed. "I can see where there'd be problems, but can't say as I've been around enough to hear of anyone with your…condition, having livestock."

The knob to the shed turned easily. The musky scent of dusty earth hit me. It was stronger than I'd ever smelled before and I couldn't tell if it was the place or my recently augmented sense of smell. Overall, the smell took me back to my childhood and the old root cellar we'd had on the ranch. There were shelves in the shed and a bare lightbulb that indicated there should be electricity run to it. A couple of outlets were near the shelves.

I started to nod to Marzie, then glanced at the cabin where Watabe stood watching us. "Should we ask to walk the property?"

"That's up to you." Marzie matched her voice to my low tones. "Some buyers do that, and some just ask where the property lines are."

"Right. Never done this before."

"Which is why you brought me along. What do you want to do?"

The day had ended up a lot longer than we'd planned. To walk the fence on fifty acres could take a little while. Vash and Garnet were waiting for dinner and the dreaded shopping. "Let's just ask. This place is within budget, right?"

Marzie nodded. "Top end, but yes. With how long it's been on the market, I can probably get a few grand knocked off."

"Good. I'll let you work your magic on that one." We headed back toward the cabin. "But this one will work just fine. Just hope Vash likes it."

"We'll see on that one." Marzie paused on the steps going back up to the backdoor as her phone rang.

At the same moment, Briar and Harris' phones rang in front of the cabin.

I felt a bit left out as I went up to Watabe. "Where are the property lines?"

He pointed toward the tree line to the south. "Just inside the trees there is a fence, a hundred yards or so beyond that is another fence. That's the south border."

"Geez." Marzie hung up. "Lucas, that was Cin, we've got a situation back at the house. Mr. Watabe, we need to go, but I'll be calling you later and letting you know what Sergeant Lucas has decided."

"Thank you. I hope everything's going to be okay." Watabe held out his hand to me. "It was nice meeting both of you."

"And you." I shook his hand. "Thanks for taking

the time to show us around."

In the front of the house, Briar's voice raised in anger. "Don't give me excuses. Find that plane before it lands and we'll be where it touches down."

Another plane coming over. A chill went through me. Did that mean the effrits had called in reinforcements? What form would they take? As Marzie said her goodbyes, I rushed through the house. Briar and Harris were already getting into the car. Not so deep inside me, my wolf stirred. Since the moon, he'd been more eager than ever to get out and hunt.

19

We were nearly back to Garnets when Briar's phone rang again. He thrust it at Harris. "Answer and put it on the speaker."

Without a word, Harris did as instructed.

"Talk to me, May, what do we have?" Briar barked.

"They're heading for a private airfield between Pueblo and Canyon City, at least that's what the seers are telling me." There was clicking in the background like she was working on a computer. Somehow Briar's magical right hand using a computer while tracking bad guys hit me as odd.

"Send me the coordinates." Briar glanced into the backseat. "Ms. Campbell, we're going on a bit of a side trip. You'll need to stay in the car."

Marzie held up her hands. "I'm not badass enough to take on effrits. I'm good staying put as long as the car doesn't explode or anything like that."

"I hope it doesn't come to that." Briar looked back at the road and changed lanes so he could take the next exit like we were heading toward Garnet's place. "May, I also need to know how that plane got past mundane authorities, and this deep into our airspace. It also managed to avoid the general magic protections we've got up on the borders. That means they're a problem."

"My question is why the plane?" May asked. "When they followed you, Lucas and Vash into the country, the effrit just flew on their own power. This might not be effrits."

"But it's tied to them, else why would it be heading this way? Work the angles."

"Will do. I just sent you the coordinates. From the look of things, you're going to be five minutes too late."

Briar growled. "Then clear the way with the local authorities. I'm about to break some speed laws." He cleared the light going into Fort Carson and hit the gas. The car vibrated as it picked up speed.

"I'll make some calls." May disconnected the call.

"Let me try to help a bit." Harris handed the phone back to me. "Answer it if she calls back."

Glad to have something to do, I took the phone.

Harris took a deep breath, started lightly chanting, and magic filled the car.

"Wow." Marzie sounded impressed by the magic he was weaving.

The way the landscape on the other side of the car window blurred, I had to turn and keep my eyes forward before I hurled. I'd gone faster in airplanes, but not on the ground.

Briar kept his hands tight on the wheel as he swung around the light traffic we encountered. The couple of stoplights we hit were miraculously green and no one seemed inclined to pull out in front of us as we shot down the highway.

My phone rang. I glanced at the screen. Garnet. "Hey, what's up?"

"Man…recept…wher…" Her words clipped in and out filled with a strange static.

"Garnet, I can't hear most of what you're saying." I wasn't sure if she could hear me either.

"Luc…some…com…defe…Va…" the call went dead.

I stared at the phone. It sounded like something was happening to Vash. I wanted to tell Briar to turn the car around and get us back to the house, but I knew Garnet's defenses were strong and should be enough to protect them. I had to trust in that. If the effrits had called in reinforcements, we had to deal with that as fast as we could.

"The magic was probably interfering with the connection." Marzie patted my leg. "We have to hope they're going to be okay. Cin and Chad are on their way to the house, Cin had a feeling they needed to be there."

She told me that as we'd left the cabin, but it helped a little hearing it again.

Harris let out a loud breath and collapsed. The seatbelt across his chest was the only thing that kept him from cracking his head on the dashboard.

"There goes our strongest magic user," Briar muttered as the car slowed just outside the city limits of Penrose. "At least he cut our journey in less than half."

Briar's phone in my hand rang. Agent May. I tapped to answer, but his phone was different than mine and I had to swipe.

"That must've been Gavin's magic that made you jump like that." She started without preamble.

"Yes, but he's out of the picture now," Briar replied as I held the phone between the seats. I knew he could hear her even without it on speaker, but figured he needed to have her hearing him.

"Okay, we've confirmed the plane appears to be on course to the airport not far from the regional prison." May paused and silence filled the line so long that I started to wonder if we'd been cut off. "It looks like something disabled the western alarm spells. I've got agents heading to the coast now to see what's going on."

"That's not good, May," Briar growled as we crossed a highway without pausing for yellow lights on both ends of the overpass. "It means they've got people over here working for them."

"Or at least with them," May corrected.

I understood the difference. It appeared that mercenaries were available in the magical world just like the mundane one, or it could've been a group with similar goals who had formed a temporary alliance with the effrits. But it made me wonder what it was with Vash that made people want her so badly.

"With your faster course, I think you're going to reach the airport a good three minutes before the plane lands."

Briar frowned. "Three minutes, it should be more than that."

"Sorry, something is pushing them along too. Might be some kind of magic. I'll work on it."

"Okay. Thanks, May. I wish you were here. We could use the extra magic."

"Understood." Again, there was a pause. "Look, I've got our agent on the coast on the other line. Gotta go."

"Track them down, May." Briar nodded as he turned off the highway onto a narrow dirt road, barely cutting his speed and fishtailing slightly.

Harris rocked in his seat, but the seatbelt continued to hold him tight.

May ended the call and I pulled the phone back across the seatback. "What are we going to do? What can we do if there's a bunch of effrits on this plane?"

Briar shook his head. "I doubt it's effrits. Mages maybe. If they hadn't triggered the ancient wards over the Grand Canyon, we wouldn't even know they were coming."

I glanced at Marzie and cocked an eyebrow. "Ancient wards over the Grand Canyon?"

"They're set in the canyon itself." Briar turned again and a landing strip came into view. "We don't know who originally set them, possibly the Anasazi. Some Navajo shamans still monitor them and warned us about them. They're still very sensitive about outsider magic crossing their borders."

"I don't doubt it."

A private plane dropped out of the cloudy sky, angling toward the airstrip. It didn't look like it could hold a lot of people, but if they were things like effrits, they could easily fit a lot of smoky bad guys in a small space.

"What do you want me to do?" My wolf was

right under my skin, ready to roar out and tear people apart.

"I think you're about to get your opportunity to try out that new gun I bought for you." Briar didn't even slow down for the open gate that marked the edge of the airfield's property. The way he roared down the road heading toward the strip I started to wonder if he was going to stop even for the airplane.

I was going to need time to get the gun case out of the back and grab ammo. I couldn't remember what Urson had loaded Stormbringer with, and hoped it would be right for whatever we were dealing with. Dirt flew as Briar spun out and whipped the car around near the small building at the end of the landing strip.

Dust wrapped itself around us as I undid my seat belt and rushed toward the back of the car. "Briar, open the trunk!"

The trunk popped open as I reached it. I moved the case with the sword aside. It wasn't as useful to me at that moment as the ammo would be. The odds were it'd be weeks or more before I totally felt comfortable with the strange weapon.

I grabbed the first box of ammo, flipped it open, and dumped it out into my hand before dropping bullets into my pocket. It wasn't a great plan, but they'd be easily accessed if I needed to reload my magazine. I was going to need to get more magazines for Stormbringer; it would make reloading a lot easier.

Briar appeared at my side. "Okay. We're going to try diplomacy first. If we're dealing with mercenaries and not zealots, they might respond to that. I can easily become the highest bidder. If they start shooting, anything, machine guns, fireballs, anything, shoot to kill."

Closing the trunk, I nodded. "Got it." It would make me feel good to take out a few terrorists and if they started shooting, that was what they were.

The plane came to a stop near the end of the strip then turned around and taxied toward the building and the several cars parked there.

Briar stood a little taller, squared his shoulders, and his wolf rose close to the surface that I was acutely aware of it there. My own wolf was pushing me on. I'd been told that under extreme stress it would be possible for me to shift when it wasn't the full moon, but I'd hoped to get a handle on that like I wanted to learn the sword before I was forced to do it.

The plane stopped a short distance from the building and as soon as its forward motion stopped, the door opened and folded down a ramp. The scent of incense and wolves hit me, the burnt smell of effrits mingled with it.

I growled and stopped a few feet behind Briar, my hand tense at my side, ready to draw on the first thing that got aggressive.

Smoke poured out of the plane, curling toward the sky.

"Bring it down!" Briar shouted and ran toward the ramp.

Not needing to be told twice, I whipped Stormbringer out and traced the track of the smoke.

With nothing solid to hit, I wasn't sure what was going to happen as I gently squeezed the trigger.

A roar like thunder rocked out of the gun as the bullet flew from the muzzle. There was a bit of a kick, but not nearly as bad as I was afraid it was going to be.

Light danced through the air as the bullet shot toward the smoke. The longer the projectile flew, the more light came toward it until lightning was arching around it. When it entered the smoke something screamed and the lighting exploded.

I grinned and stared at the gun. "Cool."

A body coalesced in the center of the smoke and I squeezed off another round.

Howling erupted from the plane before the effrit hit the ground.

Without thinking, I leveled Stormbringer and emptied the clip in a series of jerky shots. I had to stop the howling. The howling meant death. Howling had killed my unit. The plane didn't stand a chance. The lightning bullets struck in quick succession.

As the howling stopped and the plane exploded, I popped the clip and already had it half full. I had to keep the howling from starting up again. I had to keep people alive.

Cars and trucks that had been parked around the building raced away, but it didn't matter. If I kept shooting the plane, the howling wouldn't start up again.

When the clip was full again, I pointed Stormbringer at the plane and squeezed off two rounds before Briar jerked my arm up, sending the third shot high into the sky. It exploded and rained fire down on us.

"Stand down soldier!" Briar shouted and he batted tiny fireballs off his shoulder and head.

The flame of one hitting me in the head made me aware of the danger I was in. My wolf whined deep inside me. It was again afraid. I ruffled my hair, trying to make sure that the last of the fire was off me then looked at Briar. "Did we get them?"

Briar frowned. "I don't know how many of them survived and how many didn't, you made a mess, Sergeant Lucas. It would've been nice to have someone to question, but they're either dead or running."

I wasn't sure what to say. I shrugged. "The howling set me off." I let out a sigh. "This isn't going to be easy to get under control, is it?"

"Doesn't look that way." His frown deepened. "You know this makes me question the intelligence of getting you a powerful magical weapon capable of blowing things up."

"We have to keep Vash safe." As the words left my mouth, I holstered Stormbringer and whipped out my phone. "Vash." I hit the speed dial for Garnet's place.

All I got was static.

Deep inside me, my wolf unwound from its scared ball and roared through me. I shoved Briar away as the wolf burst out. I fell to the ground, but only for a moment. He filled me with the need to get to Vash. We took off running faster than I'd ever run before.

The ground was just a blur under our paws as we ran north. The speed we traveled at was breathtaking. It also helped clarify the blur of the… the… moment back at the airstrip. There had been werewolves on that plane. They'd howled, must've been changed already. Like before, the sound pushed me out of the here and now and somewhere else. Stormbringer in my hand had provided the answer as to how to make the howling stop. My reaction as Lucas had scared my wolf again, but our combined fear for Vash's safety had let us shift and become one again.

The high-desert brush we ran across, using the road to our right as a guide to where we were going, was enough cover that most people wouldn't spot us. From my years in the Army Rangers, I understood covert, and my wolf picked it up as he guided us along at top speed.

Rabbits and deer ran from us as we went, but the drive to hunt was outweighed by the need to get to Vash. Something was happening. She needed us, or she would've been there with us on the airstrip as the PTSD took over and she could've helped as she'd done previously.

We burst out of the brush onto a flat valley with

short grass. A herd of frightened pronghorns scattered from our passing. We raced past them like they'd been backing up.

As we went up yet another hill, our chest heaved from the exertion of running so far, so fast.

There was the trailer park where Garnet lived. We turned slightly so we could approach from the hillside behind the trailers. It wasn't the most direct route, but it was the safest, and the one to give us a slight edge if anyone was watching the street.

Smoke and ash filled my nostrils as we jumped the fence into Garnet's back yard.

Effrit.

Somehow, they'd found us.

Glancing around, we waited a moment before leaping onto the porch. No one was there waiting for us. There wasn't even the tingle of magic we'd begun associating with walking into Garnet's house. Something was very wrong.

The front door was ajar, so we nosed the door wide enough that we could slip into the house. The place was a wreck. Books and DVDs were scattered all over the place. Furniture lay upended. The reek of ash was so strong we gagged slightly.

Garnet's leg stuck out from under the turned-over couch. We sniffed her. Wolf sent the feeling that she was still alive.

There was no way we could move the couch without hands. With a series of pictures of what I wanted to do, I asked my wolf to give control of our body back to me.

He retreated in a wave of pain and nausea that

left me on my knees retching on Garnet's beige carpet. My body realigned, bones breaking, and reforming as I became human again. I fought back the scream that threatened to come out. I didn't remember it hurting so much the first time I'd shifted, but then I'd had Vash and two alphas at my side, coaxing me through it. On my own, I couldn't exactly remember how everything went, or how to make it easy.

Once the pain cleared, I stood and lifted the couch that felt like it weighed almost nothing, and set it back in place. Garnet still hadn't moved, but with the couch gone, I could see her ribs moving with slow, even breaths.

"Garnet?" I knelt next to her, and shook her slightly, before rolling her over.

Dark smudges covered her cut-up face. It looked like she'd been cleaning a chimney when something had rushed out to attack her.

She blinked and slowly focused on me. "Lucas, you're back. And you're naked, except for a holster." She eased to a sitting position. "You might want to go get some pants on."

Pants. That would explain the soft draft I felt. I touched Stormbringer's wooden handle. How had I lost my pants but not my gun? That didn't make sense.

"Where's Vash?"

Garnet shook her head. "They took her. Had some kind of magic that trapped her in a bottle."

I patted my leg. Her bell. Where was her bell? It had been in my pants when I'd shifted. Was it lying on the warm dark asphalt of the airstrip? Had someone else claimed it? I had to get it back.

"How... ?"

"Pants." Garnet pointed down the hall. "Go get some pants on. Now." She eased back against the couch.

I almost argued that pants weren't important, finding Vash was, but I turned and hurried to my room and yanked out a pair of clean jeans and put them on, after I'd taken off the gun belt, then grabbed a T-shirt too and pulled it on before refastening Stormbringer around my waist. There was no way I was going to let the gun get away from me. I might need it. It didn't matter that I didn't have a full clip, any edge the gun could give me, I was going to take.

I made it back to the living room as the front door burst open and Kilkari and his wife stormed in.

"Is everyone alright?" Cin asked, taking everything in quickly.

"Effrit," Kilkari growled.

"They have Vash." I put my hand on my weapon. Although I wasn't thinking about drawing on either one of them, the gesture made me feel better, more in control.

"Then we get her back." Cin went to Garnet. "We just have to find them. Garnet, did they say anything that might help?"

Garnet shook her head. "Not really. They are very quiet, and I think that makes them scarier."

"I could see that." Cin settled on the couch next to Garnet. "Where are Briar, Gavin, and Marzie?"

I shrugged. "Last I saw them they were at a small community airport south of here. I kinda lost it, blew up the plane, then realized Vash was in danger and ran here.”

Kilkari got a thoughtful look, then his eyes widened. “The closest community airport is down outside Florence. You ran from Florence? You have to be exhausted.”

“Yeah, but finding Vash is more important, right?” I had no doubt that once the adrenalin wore off, I was going to hit the ground hard, and I hoped it would last long enough for us to locate Vash. There was no way I was going to leave her with the effrits.

“Right.” Cin nodded, and patted Garnet’s leg. “Okay. Until we know what Agent Briar and company are planning, we’ve got to go ahead and start working on things of our own. Garnet, we’re going to need the locals. I felt a really powerful magical entity right before we arrived. Since I haven’t felt that before, we have to assume that they’re involved in this somehow.”

I nodded and glanced at the recliner. The soft chair called me to sit down, but I resisted the urge. “That makes sense.”

“Good. We’re going to need to see if we can get other magic users moving and try to triangulate on this powerful person.” Cin pulled out her phone. “Garnet, let’s make some calls and see what we can get moving.”

Garnet glanced around, then stood and headed for the kitchen. “Let me find my phone.”

“All I was getting was static when trying to call from the airstrip.” I pulled out my phone and frowned. The battery was dead. “This doesn’t make sense, I charged it last night."

Kilkari nodded. "It does when you stop and realize that magic and technology don't get along." Then he wrinkled his face. "Wait a minute. How did you get your phone back here when you shifted and ran?"

I paused. I'd thought I'd shoved the phone in my pants pocket, maybe I'd slipped it in the holster with Stormbringer. "The gun holster?"

"The gun and holster have the magic to shift with you?" Kilkari whistled. "Man, I'm going to see what Urson will charge me for a setup that will do that."

"Might help us keep track of you on full-moon nights." Cin frowned at her phone. "Still getting static on the phone."

I frowned. "In Afghanistan, something cut out wireless communications for two weeks. Is it possible this is connected? Could our power magical entity be responsible?"

Chad looked at Cin who shrugged. "Maybe," he muttered.

"Then let's see if the internet is working." Garnet came out of the kitchen frowning at her own phone. "Maybe I can chat with enough people to get something going."

"See what you can do." I turned and walked out onto the porch. At least the smell of the effrits wasn't as strong there reminding me of my failure. I didn't like the thought that something that had been in the desert had followed us to the states and had stolen Vash. Sure it tied things together, but I didn't like it.

Kilkari followed me out. "You okay?"

I shook my head. "No. That being of light back in Afghanistan trusted me to take care of her and I've lost her." My heart pounded as I leaned against the rickety porch railing. Saying it made me angry. If I'd let Vash go with us house hunting and to visit Urson, I'd have been with her with the effrits came but I'd thought she'd be safer staying home. I'd also put Garnet in danger. People around me weren't supposed to be in danger, they were supposed to be protected.

"Sometimes things get out of hand, I understand that." Kilkari crossed his arms and started to lean on the railing, and when it creaked really loudly, straightened and frowned. "We've got a good group of people around us, we'll all work together and find Vash before those effrits can do anything more to her."

"I hope you're right." I let out a long breath.

Something tingled with magic and we both turned to the patch of yard just off the porch. A soft glow burst into being. I pulled Stormbringer and leveled it at the glow.

Agent Briar stepped through with his hands raised. "Lower your weapon, Lucas. It's just us."

Behind him, Harris, Marzie, and Agent May stepped from the glow into the side yard.

I lowered Stormbringer but didn't relax. There was no way I was going to relax until we had Vash back.

21

Agent Briar glared at his phone as we all walked into the house. "I don't know what's going on with the tech."

"Luckily it's just phones." Cin looked up from the table where she had a laptop out and going. "Can't explain it, but the internet is working just fine."

"Must be air magic." Agent May hurried over to the table and glanced down. "It's hitting wireless communication, but not wired. I've read some theories about using it this way, but haven't seen it in action."

"Is there a way to counter it?" I was learning that most magic had a counter if anyone had ever thought of one.

"That will take time." Briar started pacing. "I've got illegal supernaturals in the middle of the U.S. and they've brought more in and stolen a very powerful asset. We don't have time to chase magical theories."

Although I didn't like the idea of Vash being referred to as an asset, I was with him on not having time.

"Air magic makes sense." Cin stared at her computer. "Garnet, when you can, start reaching out to your coven, maybe if we switch to wired internet, we can beat these guys. Anyone still have a wired phone? That might be faster than emails."

"How many network connections to we need?" Garnet came down the hall carrying coiled wires. "I've only got so many ports on my router."

"I wonder if telepaths would help." Harris, still looking like something someone had run over then thrown into a river, made it to a recliner, and plopped down.

"Telepaths?" Agent May straightened. "Maybe. Do you know a network? The closest one I'm aware of is in operating out of DC."

"Sure, there's a few here in the springs. Garnet, you remember them, we met them at that last community pot luck." Harris put his head down and was rubbing his temples as he spoke.

"Yeah." Garnet handed the network cables to me. "Give me a minute and I'll get an email off. Hope they don't take forever to get back to us."

"We don't have forever," Briar reiterated. "But having a telepath with our search parties could be helpful."

I held up the cables. "Who needs network?"

May pulled out a laptop from her shoulder bag. "Give me one. Let me see what I can do. Maybe if we can figure out the area this air spell is covering that will give us an idea."

A sly grin spread across my face as I handed her a cable. "If it's centered on the caster, then we plot it out and head for the center to take them out. Hopefully, the caster has Vash."

"Right." May took the cable and plugged it into

her laptop. "And while Cin and Garnet are working with the local mages and telepaths to triangulate on the powerful mage, we can be doubly sure that we've got the right spot."

Briar took a seat on the couch next to Kilkari. "And then there's the times when werewolves are just the regulated muscle to the mages."

I spun toward him. "Was that why there were werewolves on that plane? They were someone's muscle?" Guards. That was something I could understand. It also told me that magic users weren't as all-powerful as they appeared to be.

"And if you hadn't run off, you could've helped us kick his butt." Briar took a long breath. "As it was, he came pretty close to kicking our collective butts. If you hadn't blown up his plane, then his pack would've torn us apart."

That didn't sound like the same kind of arrangement I'd seen so far in the states, or at least not with Mark and Urson. "He's commanding a pack of wolves?"

"We don't know for sure. We took down two wolves, and he nearly took us down. There were another six wolves in the plane that hadn't survived you blowing it up." Briar stood and fiddled with something on his chest. It looked like he was trying to unfasten a belt, then the sword Urson had given me appeared as he got the belt undone and pulled it free.

Kilkari whistled. "Is that the sword Urson was making for you? I've seen some of his other work, but never anything that could turn invisible like that. Where's the gun?"

I touched Stormbringer's handle, amazed that I could see it, and apparently, others couldn't. "Right here." I gently pulled it free and showed it to him.

"Sweet." Kilkari picked it up with hesitant fingers. "Heavy. Is this how you blew up the plane?"

"That and magic bullets." In any other gathering of people, I'd have felt silly talking about such things.

Kilkari turned toward the kitchen. "Cin, we've gotta get some of these."

Cin frowned at him. "You've got fangs and claws, I've got spells. You know I'm not a fan of firearms, when we can avoid them."

"Right. But it turns invisible and shoots magic bullets. I bet it could even bring down aliens." He frowned slightly as he handed the gun back to me.

I cocked an eyebrow. "Aliens?"

"Long story, but yes, aliens." Kilkari had a slightly reluctant look as his fingers left the sidearm.

"Okay, guys, enough gun talk for the moment. Put it all back in your pants." Garnet stood from the table. "We've got a couple of telepaths heading this way to keep us connected, but they have a limited range, so we can't cast our net too far."

Feeling better with Stormbringer back in my hand, I slipped it into its holster. "What's too far?"

"We don't know yet." Garnet popped the keyboard off her laptop and laid the display on the table. "Come take a look."

"I've got a response back from Landon Weir, the druid in Divide." Cin stood and leaned over the display. "He says the source of the power is northeast of his location. He figured it's between him and the

Air Force Academy, maybe even him and Colorado Springs depending on the angle."

Harris hobbled over to the table and leaned slightly as if to get a better look. "Do we know if the air spell is affecting wireless communications up there?"

Cin nodded. "Yes, he said cell phones, wireless networks, and walkie-talkies are down. He's not sure about anything else. Should I tell him to head toward the powerful mage?"

Briar stood and rubbed his face. "He's a druid. If I remember right, his husband is a badger, but also with Colorado Parks and Wildlife."

"That's right." Garnet nodded. "Lucas, Vash, and I ran into Brock at the store the other day."

"That big blond guy? He's a badger?" I looked at Briar. "You guys really need to get some kind of newbie handbook done up to make things easier for some of us."

"Problem with that is things like books can slip the oath." Briar shook his head. "We haven't figured out how to include them so we can safely create something like that. For now, it's an as-needed thing."

"Right." I got that sensitive info had to be kept secret, but being able to sit down and read about things I might run into would be really handy. Sure, I was a werewolf and had already met a bear shifter, so a badger shifter shouldn't be a huge jump, but it hit me as odd. My whole life was getting odder by the minute. Having a handbook would make my life simpler.

"A drawback too, would be how large the book would need to be even if we just had a page per strange thing." Harris chuckled. "We've got sources once we get clearance for such things. Who knows, we might even end up with a weird wiki or something like that."

Cin started to say something, then glanced at Briar and turned back to her computer. "I'll let Landon know to head out and we'll try and meet up with him. Hopefully, he's sensitive enough for the telepaths to connect to."

"Tell him to be careful." Briar straightened. "We don't the extent of the effrits' capabilities, nor do we know what the mage who landed in Florence can do, or exactly how they fit together."

"Will do." Cin tapped away on her keyboard.

Garnet straightened from her laptop display. "Okay. I've got one of the telepaths coming here and the others are fanning out along the foothills. Sorry, I can't get one from Woodland Park, or anywhere else west of the peak."

"With phones down, it'll have to do." Briar leaned against one of the chairs at the table. A muffled chime came from his pocket.

"Vash's bell." I stared at him. "It was in my pocket when I shifted."

He reached into his own pocket and pulled it out. "It was. Luckily it didn't melt when the car was blown up."

A cooling, quiet feeling flooded through me as I cradled the bell in my palm. It was too light for Vash to be in it, and colder than it had ever been, but I had it. Soon I'd have Vash back too and everything would be okay. "Thanks." I closed my fingers over it and stood there while others worked around me. Even my wolf felt a little more content have some part of her back in our possession.

"Okay—" Agent May stood from her seat and pulled Garnet's display toward her "—from what I've been able to determine by getting into the local phone networks, here's the area affected by the outage." She pinched her hands together on the screen to zoom it out, then drew a line with her finger. "Some of it might be a little off, but it's a starting point."

I stared at the screen. The area was huge. It stretched from south of Pueblo to the southern edge of Denver and out onto the plains east of Colorado Springs while reaching deep into the mountains. It would take us days to search all of it, but if we were right, we weren't going to have to.

"The center is here." May tapped a spot just north of Pikes Peak.

Harris and Garnet shared a questioning glance. "That's right where a major fire went through a few years ago," they said in unison.

"A fire?" Briar frowned as he looked at the map on the display. "Effrits and a fire. That doesn't sound like a coincidence."

"And there was a hushed report that the fire might've been an act of terrorism since some reports had been found that said the terrorists could strike major blows against the U.S. by hitting targets like national forests." Kilkari shook his head as he looked at the map.

"That's right." I turned away from the table. "I was part of the group that found that intel. I never realized it was actually put into play. Some targets aren't normally hit because they may or may not cause major impacts."

"This one did major damage," Harris muttered. "Not lots of lives lost, but property damage was extensive, and it impacted the area for several years with flash floods and such. I think they just recently opened most of the burn scar to limited hiking and camping. I haven't been up there yet to see how bad it is."

"Looks like we're heading that way now." I picked up the sword from the coffee table where Briar had laid it. I still wasn't sure if it would be of any help, but the bad guys had Vash, and I was bloody well going to use anything I had to bring them down.

22

Garnet's little purple car wasn't designed to hold the people we had crammed into it, and it didn't have the clearance to easily get down the rut-filled dirt road we drove along trying to get to the center of the air spell. I hoped the Kilkaris, Harris, and the telepath were having an easier go of it in Kilkari's SUV behind us. The slow travel made me grumpy, as did the intense closeness of my wolf. He felt ready to burst out of my skin and start rending people. I was itchier than I had been the night of the full moon.

I couldn't stop the growl that came out when I hit my head on the top of the car again as Garnet took a rut too hard and we all got bounced around hard.

"Easy there, Lucas," Briar had a growl in his own tone in the front seat.

"Sorry, but Purple Rain isn't designed for off-roading." Garnet apologized for the umpteenth time. "I know this is a road and everything, but just barely."

"You're doing your best, Garnet." Agent May patted her shoulder. "We're getting close."

Garnet nodded. "I know. I can feel them. I'm going to get those effrits, so help me, goddess." Her hands were so tight on the steering wheel they had to be hurting.

"We'll make them all regret setting foot on our soil." Briar braced himself against the dashboard, giving me a warning of another rut coming up. "We're going to need to turn left soon. At least that's what that telepath says."

Garnet shook her head. "Left? Are you sure you got that correct? We turn left and we're going off a cliff."

Briar tensed up. "Yes, he said left, but I'm thinking this is the point where we leave the vehicles behind and go on foot."

"I think there's a pull-off up ahead." Garnet pointed off to the right. "We just stop here and leave the cars blocking the road and the sheriff's department is going to get involved and we don't need anyone else up here right now."

"Correct, which is why we closed the road in both directions." Agent Briar left scratches in the dash as we bounced around again. "But there are still hikers and campers up here from before we closed the road. We're going to have to watch out for them."

"Special treatment thanks to strings we can pull," May added. "Comes in handy a lot of the time."

"Helps people like Kilkari get off when they kill people too." I was still amazed they'd been able to cover up for him like that. Sure, Agent Briar's taskforce was officially part of the FBI, although they were actually a totally separate covert group, and I'd seen plenty of covert cover-ups over the years, but killing a sheriff sounded incredible.

"Our string-pulling might pay off for you one of these days too, Sergeant Lucas." Briar didn't turn and look at me, but I could tell it wasn't a good time to bring up something like that. We were all on edge. The musky scent of wolf filled the little car, telling me his wolf was as close to bursting forth as mine. It wouldn't do Vash any good if we both lost it. We had to hold it together to save her.

"Here's the pull-off." Garnet swung the car into the spot where there were already two big trucks, and just enough room for us and Kilkari to park.

"Civilians." Agent Briar growled as he opened the door. "We're going to have to watch out for them."

"Then we will," May countered a little sharper than I was used to hearing her speak to Briar. "It's what we do."

We were all more on edge than I had realized. That wasn't good. A team needed to be as focused as possible when going into an unknown situation. The more stressed we all were, the greater the probability of mistakes. We didn't need mistakes. The other problem was other than the agents and the couples we didn't know the real extent of what the others were capable of. Lack of knowledge also made things dangerous.

"They're that way." Garnet pointed across the road as everyone in the Kilkari's SUV got out and joined us at the back of her car.

"Right." Cin looked down the slope where green covered the ground, but all the trees were nothing but blackened skeletons of what they had been before the fire had gone through.

I couldn't see anything but more rocks, scrub,

and burnt trees. It didn't make sense.

"I might be more useful with paws." Kilkari walked back to his vehicle and started taking off his clothes.

"It's good you don't do this in town all the time." Cin walked over and looked like she was being a somewhat visible shield for him to change behind. Anyone on the other side of us would have an unobstructed view as he tossed his clothes into the SUV then his body flowed like warm putty until a black wolf shook between the cars. He shook like he'd just gotten out of water. When he finished, he nosed Cin before striding up to Agent Briar. There was a level of confidence in his motions that I was jealous of. How long was it going to take me before I could shift like that? Sure, it sounded like my last shift to wolf had been fairly quick and easy, but my wolf had overtaken me. The change back hadn't been so easy. This looked like Kilkari and his wolf had an easy understanding, making the change easy for both of them.

"Alright, unless we've got other shifts to do, let's get this going." Cin looked from me to Agent Briar.

I patted Stormbringer. "Still more comfortable with guns over claws." As the words left me, I wondered if there would come a day when that wouldn't be true. Would my bond with my wolf become such that we could be more dangerous than bullets or blades? I wasn't sure how I would feel about that when, or if, it happened.

Agent Briar shook his head. "I'm hoping to interrogate someone. That'll be hard to do in fur."

The telepath, a skinny kid named Mac, sighed. "Guys, we've got another team heading east from up there." He pointed southwest of our pull-off. "I haven't met them, but they're focused on finding the powerful magic-user."

"That would probably be Brock and Landon." Harris put a hand over his eyes like it would help him see them. "They were coming down from Divide. They're probably more at home in this terrain than we are. We need to get moving."

"I'll let them know we're here and heading in." Mac closed his eyes for a moment, then opened them back up. "The druid said he's got eyes on a group of effrit, and some people he can't identify."

Briar headed across the road. "I don't like the sound of that. Come on folks, we need to get moving."

Kilkari took point, and I followed his bushy black tail. The going was rough but reminded me of some of the mountain canyons my brother and I had spent time in while we were growing up. Of course, in those days the trees there had been full of leaves and needles, not the blackened corpses we were having to navigate through, but the steepness and promise of rolling down to the bottom of the hill were similar. Maybe, after we survived and got everyone home safe, I'd bring Vash up here and go hiking, or better yet, take her to the family ranch and introduce her to Mom and Lyle. I hoped she would like it, and the house Ms. Campbell had found for us.

Above us, a golden eagle banked, screamed once, and flew in the direction we were going.

After a moment, Mac pointed toward the dot the bird had become. "Follow the eagle. He… sorry, she, will lead us where we need to go."

I stared at the bird, then back at Briar. "Are there eagle shifters too?"

He frowned. "Yes, but that's not one of them. I think it might be Weir's familiar.

"You're right." Garnet stopped her downward climb and steadied herself on a tree. "Her name is Frigga. She's huge." Then she pulled her hand back and stared at it before rubbing it on the jeans she'd changed into before heading out. Her efforts left black streaks on the faded denim. "Okay, folks, don't grab the trees unless you want soot on your hands. This is gross."

"If we'd known we'd be hiking this afternoon, we'd have brought walking sticks." Cin looked like she was about to touch on of the charred trees, then avoided it.

Agent May, Cin, and Garnet all stopped and stared with blank looks.

"Someone's doing something," Harris muttered. "We need to get moving."

Kilkari shook himself again, then took off running with Agent Briar trotting behind him. We'd be stronger the more people we had when we encountered the bad guys. I stopped and looked back at the mages and telepath.

"Go." Cin shooed me on. "We're right behind you. Keep Chad safe."

It wasn't the answer I wanted, but it would do.

The slope was not one I would've dreamed about

running down a month earlier, but my reflexes had improved a lot. With my wolf lingering so close to my skin, it felt like I was anticipating every slip and slide as we went. Kilkari had no trouble navigating the passage on four paws, but even with our enhancements, Briar and I still slid and stumbled from time to time. The footing wasn't the best; sometimes the green scrub hid problem spots and holes, but every time it felt like I was going to fall, my body adjusted ever so slightly to keep me upright.

Something ahead of us tingled of magic. The temperature rose, reminding me of some of my days in the desert. Sweat flowed down my face, stinging my eyes. It was something my wolf didn't know how to deal with. I blinked frantically and cleared it.

Something big moved to my right, sending up a cloud of dust.

I turned as a huge blond beast ran toward us. He was broad of shoulder, covered in blond hair, his face an angled snout with a white stripe running from pale nostrils back under his eyes.

"Keep going," Agent Briar urged. "It's just Officer Summers. We'll make introductions later."

Summers, the man I'd met in the store who was a badger shifter. He looked more like some kind of mutant bear, not a badger. Was it possible that he could stop his shift and not become a full badger?

A man came running down the same slope, moving slightly slower. He had a rifle slung over one shoulder and a staff in his hand. He was going to cross our path shortly. I hoped he was the druid everyone'd been talking about. The eagle swooped down from the sky and flew above his head for a moment before taking off past Officer Summers.

Kilkari slid to a stop and started to raise his muzzle to the sky, then stopped and looked back at me.

I nodded at him. "Thanks." I wouldn't be any good to Vash if the equivalent of friendly fire took out my ability to be of help. I was going to need to do what I could to get my PTSD under control, but that was going to have to wait for another day.

We stopped on the edge of a crater, at least that's what it looked like to me. A deep hole that looked like an asteroid had punched a hole in the hillside. The lack of charred trees and scrub made me wonder if this was where the fire had started, or had this land been this way longer than that? Down in the middle, a tall man with long black hair and an almost equally long beard stood shaking a soda bottle. Two effrits waited patiently behind him, and two men stood in front of him.

I froze and growled. One of the men was Rob Colfax, beta of the Denver pack. What was he doing standing talking to a man torturing Vash? She had to be in the soda bottle. I could almost make out the soft tingle of her bell-like voice calling for help.

"This complicates things," Agent Briar muttered. "Kilkari, take down Colfax. Try to leave him able to answer questions. Everyone else, we need that bottle."

"Got it." The druid, Weir, panted slightly as he stopped next to us. "Brock and I will take on one of the effrits first."

"We'll get the other one," Cin sounded out of breath as the others caught up to us.

Not bothering to stifle another growl, I focused on the bearded man and pulled out Stormbringer. I took a steadying breath. Holding it together was going to be important. I couldn't save Vash if I lost it. Years of training kicked in and everything around me fell away. Time slowed until it was just me and my target. I'd reloaded Stormbringer before leaving Garnet's house and had a couple of backup clips ready to slide in when I needed them. Thankfully, Briar had rescued the ammo from the car, like he had Vash's bell.

Around me, the others moved and I gently squeezed the trigger with the side of the man's head in my sights. The bullet should go in right above his slightly pointed ear and blow his brains out the far side of his skull, if the magic targeting worked right.

True to her name, Stormbringer cracked like thunder. The bullet flew true, then exploded less than a foot from the target.

The man turned and glared at me as he stopped shaking the bottle. His free hand started glowing and I had no idea what he was about to do as I squeezed off another shot.

23

The mage's fireball stopped only two feet in front of me. It struck a shield and blazed so bright I had to blink away the stars that filled my vision.

I had to stop firing until I could see. If there was one thing I didn't want to do it was hurt any of the people helping me get Vash back.

When I could see again, the scene was chaos, but I kept my focus on the man holding the bottle who was like a boulder in a stream, standing there calmly gesturing with his glowing hand. I turned my focus from his head to his hand. Maybe if I changed targets, I'd get him to make a mistake.

Lightning danced out of the next bullet Stormbringer flung into the fray. It cracked and sizzled, barely missing the man's fingers. It exploded when it struck the hillside behind the effrits, sending dirt and dust flying high into the air, temporarily making it hard to see much beyond the dust and dirt filling the air.

One of the effrits screamed. The sound was eerie and sent chills through me.

"The sword," Agent Briar said from my side. "It cut him at the airfield after you ran off."

I didn't feel real confident with the sword.

Stormbringer was so much more suited to me. "Okay." I nodded and started to where the man had been moments before. I kept my firearm out as long as I could.

The man who'd been standing next to Colfax rushed me, swinging a glowing sword. I spun toward him and fired.

I'd heard of silly Hollywood stunts where people could block a bullet with a sword, but had never dreamed I'd actually see it in action. That glowing sword came down in an arch and intercepted my bullet, cutting it in half. The bullet turned to ice as sleet and snow fell to the ground in front of the man.

Not pausing, and hoping I could shoot faster than he could swing, I fired three more shots in rapid succession.

Somehow the man managed to block two of them before the third caught him in the shoulder.

He didn't go down. Snarling, he pointed the sword and shouted something in a language I didn't understand. Magic like a huge invisible hand slammed into me. I flew back several feet, passing Agent Briar as I went.

"Well shit." When I stopped rolling and regained my feet, I holstered Stormbringer and pulled out the sword. If I had to go blade to blade with the man I was going to lose, but unless I got lucky again, I wasn't going to land another shot on him.

Holding the sword like a short lance, I screamed and ran at him.

The swordsman took a braced stance and held his sword up, like he was waiting to hit me hard as I ran into him.

Then he jerked.

Briar's gun barked three more times as the man fell to the ground. "Thanks for distracting him for me."

I shifted slightly and continued my run, just aiming at the long-haired man holding the bottle, hoping Briar was right and the sword could get through his defenses. Urson had crafted the sword to handle effrits and djinns. If he were one of those, maybe it could deal with his magic where my bullets weren't as effective. At least he didn't have a sword of his own.

With Briar firing and running at my side, I rushed in.

Bouncing off the mage's shield, Briar's bullets were even less effective than mine. One of them even caught me in the side. The pain barely registered.

I nearly cheered as I ran past the point where bullets bounced and nearly caught the mage in the stomach if he hadn't side-stepped at the last minute as a blade of blue flames appeared in his hand. The blade swung toward my back, but somehow I spun around and managed to block the blow.

"I don't like that sword." The man spat out as he awkwardly brought his sword up again and swung it toward me. I had no doubt that if he wasn't holding onto the bottle, he'd have been hitting me faster and harder than I could handle.

Like it had a mind of its own, the sword swung up to block again.

The blue flames of the mage's sword licked

around my sword that was glowing brighter by the second.

A scream shredded the air as the eagle grabbed hold of the bottle and yanked it free of the man before taking off downhill, flying so fast she was out of sight in seconds.

The mage stared for a moment.

I used the opportunity to bring my sword up in a tight arch. It caught the mage in the wrist, cutting his hand from his arm. He wouldn't hold Vash in a bottle without that hand.

It was his turn to scream.

A blast of magic caught me in the chest and sent me flying past the others fighting with the mage's men. When I landed in the dirt, agony lashed through my back. I staggered to my feet, without a sword in my hand. I glanced around but couldn't find it. Pulling out Stormbringer, I wondered how well his magic was going to work for him without a hand.

His blood dripped on the ground as he stalked toward me, still impervious to Agent Briar's bullets.

I started firing Stormbringer as he got closer. At least the magic bullets didn't go flying off in all directions, dangers to the people around us. They exploded when they struck his shield.

"Sergeant Lucas," his voice carried across the battlefield. "You and your unit were such a disappointment to me. You should've died in the desert with them, not come into possession of something I've been searching to destroy for centuries. The light gods smile on you, but no more. When I finish you, I'll find that damned bird and retrieve the abomination so she can be destroyed as she should've been so long ago."

"Fuck you." I squeezed the trigger, but just got a loud click. My magazine was empty. It wasn't like me to lose count of bullets. I frantically thrust my hand in my pocket to pull out a fresh magazine as I fingered the release to eject the empty one.

Magic hit me again, but it wasn't hard enough to send me flying. I stumbled back a couple of steps. Deep inside me, my wolf growled and pushed to come out. Swords and bullets had proven ineffective; maybe claws and fangs would work better.

My hands shook as I got the magazine free of my pocket. I had to hold it together. If fangs and claws were the way to go, Briar would've shifted already.

"You're a tough man, Sergeant Lucas." His remaining hand continued to glow with magic. "You could've been a great asset in your own way. Now it's time for you to die. Maybe the next Army Ranger unit I encounter will prove worthy of the name."

I slammed my fresh magazine into Stormbringer and brought the gun up. "Fuck you, asshole!"

With steady motions, I squeezed off two shots. The bullets cracked out of the barrel.

Somehow, he managed to block the shots and they exploded so quickly their concussion waves hurled the two of us and Agent Briar backward.

I jumped to my feet and glanced around. The man was gone.

"Where?" I turned, keeping Stormbringer pointed out, ready to fire if a target presented itself.

The fights were dying down. The effrits were

fading swirls of smoke the magic users were doing their best to keep from escaping. Kilkari stood over the body of a red wolf that had to be Colfax. Blood dripped from his muzzle as he shook his head before shifting back to his human form.

With a scream, the eagle drew my gaze up as she swooped low and dropped the bottle.

Suddenly not caring, I let go of Stormbringer so I could catch the bottle. The gun clattered to the ground as I caught the green plastic bottle that weighed more than it should've.

My hands shook as I unscrewed the cap. "Vash, you're safe now."

Her smoke was a bright purple and it spilled out of the bottle, then she solidified with her arms wrapped around my neck. "Lucas, you saved me!" The sparks from her hair cascaded around us.

I hugged her back. "Of course, Vash." My throat tightened and she clung to me.

In all my years, I'd never had such an end to a fight before. I fought to be strong as water filled my eyes. It had been so close. The man had been torturing Vash. Other than the night the wolves had attacked my unit, I'd never come so close to losing a fight, or someone I cared about.

24

I stood in the doorway while Vash dashed into the empty bedroom of the house I'd signed the final paperwork on the previous evening. It had taken longer than I'd hoped, and I was pretty sure Garnet was ready to get us out of her hair, although she'd never said a harsh word and seemed to enjoy having Vash around.

"This is my space?" Vash turned around with her arms spread, spinning the purple skirt she had on and sending sparks flying around the place.

"It is, do you like it?" I leaned against the door frame and couldn't help but smile at how happy she was.

She looked at me and grinned while nodding. "I do. It's bigger than my first holder's entire home, but things have changed much in the past two thousand years."

"That they have. We're going to need to get you some furniture and things to hang on the walls."

"Garnet showed me how to shop online. That way we don't have to worry about anyone finding us." She ran over to the window and hopped up on the sill, looking out into the front yard. "I can see the peak from here."

I wasn't sure my bank account was going to be able to handle Garnet teaching Vash to shop online, but she was right, it would help keep us safe from prying eyes. Vash had gotten good at casting illusions to keep her sparks from showing too much, and from what Cin and Harris said, she was good at shielding, hopefully keeping her safe from any magic users who might be looking for her.

The doorbell rang and I turned toward the front of the house.

"I'll get it." Vash vanished in a puff of smoke and seconds later, the soft creak of the door opening reached me.

I knew most people would oil that hinge, but it wasn't overly loud, and it would help me hear when the door was opened.

The musky scent of wolf and the slight herby scent of witch hit me as I strode into the living room, already knowing who to expect.

The Kilkaris stood in the entryway. Cin smiled at Vash as she handed her a small wrapped box. "It's a housewarming gift."

Vash turned and looked at me with confusion written across her delicate features. "Is our home cold? I could warm it."

Kilkari laughed. "No, sweetie, she means it's a present for your new home. We call it a housewarming because it's a new house and everything you add to it makes it more yours, and warmer."

"Oh." Vash held the box and didn't look like she totally understood the concept. I figured there were going to be cultural things that she just wouldn't get for a while.

"Unwrap it and see what it is," I urged as I waved them into the rest of the house. "You guys are going to have to bear with us, we still need to get furniture."

"But we're going to order things online and have it delivered." Vash tore into the wrapping, and I figured opening packages for kids was the same no matter where they were from or how old they were.

"Maybe we can work on that tonight." Cin patted her shoulder bag, where her laptop was. It made me wonder if she was going to be as dangerous as Garnet in introducing Vash to the modern world. "I bet we can even talk Lucas into leaving us a credit card to use."

"Maybe." I wanted to frown, but I couldn't bring myself to. For the first time in years, I had a home. Sure, it wasn't what I had expected, or how I expected, but it was a house and land, and Vash was going to make it into a real home.

Cin flashed me a mischievous grin and waved a finger at me. "We'll talk before you and Chad head out to the mountains."

"You're doomed, Bud, give it up. Between the two of them, they're after your cash." Kilkari laughed. "Just be sure to give them a total less than what's on the card before we leave, that way you can afford food and gas for the month."

"I'm not that bad." Cin put her hands on her hips and fixed her husband with a stern glare.

He smiled back and she instantly softened. "No, you're not, Dear."

"Okay. We've got a few minutes." Kilkari looked at his watch. "I told Brock we'd meet him at noon. He said he knew just the spot we could go where we won't be disturbed. He'll be going with us. More to keep an eye on us than anything. As a born shifter, he doesn't worry much about the full moon."

"Still sorting all that out." I shook my head. "Although it makes a bit of sense, there being differences between people who were born this way and people who were turned, but something like the moon not affecting them seems odd." A lot of what I was being submerged in was odd.

The doorbell rang again.

I'd been so wrapped up in talking that I hadn't heard a car coming down the drive.

"What is it?" Vash held up wall hanging that had an owl on it and something I couldn't make out written across the bottom.

"It's a wall hanging." Cin walked over held it up for her. "You put it in the entryway so people will see it when they come in."

I opened the door. Harris and Garnet stood there. Garnet had a crockpot in her hands and Harris held a couple of camping chairs.

"You're still here?" Harris raised an eyebrow. "Figured you and Chad would be on your way to the wilds already."

"Soon." I stepped aside so they could come in. "Guess it takes more than just Cin for babysitting."

Vash came over with the wall hanging. "This goes over here. There's an alarm spell on it." She held it up to the blank wall, pressed it against the sheetrock wall, and when she took her hands away, it stayed in place.

"That's very pretty, sweetie." Garnet headed for the kitchen. "Come help me get this plugged in so we can have dinner later."

"Lucas is going to give Cin his credit card so we can order furniture tonight." Vash babbled as they went.

My stomach knotted a bit thinking of what my bank balance was going to look like after a full moon of them shopping.

"Have we heard anything from Agent Briar recently?" Harris closed the front door.

"He's still trying to track down the mage who seemed to be controlling everything." I held out a hand to relieve Harris of a chair. "He said something about him either using a portal to leave the country or he's still here and hiding."

I unfolded the chair.

Harris did the same with the one he carried. "If he managed to make a portal that crosses an ocean, he's one badass mage. I've never heard of anyone doing that before. If he could, then why did he fly over in the first place?"

"A very good question." Kilkari crossed his arms.

"I've been studying portals since they used them," Cin spoke up. "They are limited and things like major rivers, lakes, or oceans can shorten the distance they can be used at. He could've used it to slip into a side dimension like Faerie, but those leave a distinct signature. There might be another answer, but I haven't stumbled on it yet."

"But we're going to spend the night shielding this place so you don't have to worry about anyone just popping in," Harris took over the discussion. "We'll also make sure everything is something Vash can reinforce and such, so she'll have control of the magic around here."

"It'll be nice for someone to." I didn't feel ready to even advise on the magic used around me. But having my… our new friends show up to make sure everything was good made me feel happy.

A soft beeping came from Kilkari as Vash and Garnet came back from the kitchen. "We need to get going."

I stared at him. "You set an alarm for when we needed to leave?"

"For ten minutes before we need to leave. I know how witches can talk and how easy it is for them to slow me down." He laughed. "I'll go get Cin's camping gear out of the car since there aren't beds here yet."

"Thanks for remembering, Honey." Cin grinned at him, then held out her hand to me. "Now, if we're going to remedy your lack of furniture, I need your card and the pertinent information to use it."

As Kilkari and Harris headed out the door, Marzie came in carrying another crockpot. "I'm not late, am I?"

"Nope right on time." Cin kept her hand out while I got my wallet from my back pocket and pulled a debit card free.

"Let me get a piece of paper to give you the

address and such." I handed her the card, then turned toward the kitchen. I thought I'd seen some of the real estate swag left behind in there.

As Marzie plugged in her crockpot next to Garnet's, I found what I was looking for and quickly jotted everything down for Cin. My skin started to itch slightly as I walked back to the living room. My wolf was trying to remind me it was time to hit the road. The moon was coming and he wanted to run.

After giving Cin the paper, I undid my gun belt and handed it to her. "I know you're not big on firearms, but I think this is probably safer with you tonight. I'd hate to have an… incident and accidentally hurt someone."

She took Stormbringer and nodded. "I'll keep it and all of you safe. Chad had a hard-enough time explaining everything to Mark after killing Rob. I'd hate to be explaining to him how things changed again."

I nodded. If there was one thing I understood it was the way the pack hierarchy worked. Kilkari had disrupted that by killing Colfax, even if he hadn't meant to. Afterward, Mark had been angry about that, until an investigation into Colfax's apartment and bank account showed he'd taken a lot of money from a bank in the Cayman Islands. The account was the only lead Agent Briar had as to who our mystery mage was and he was still trying to work that, but it was slow going. Mark had apologized for Colfax's actions and given Kilkari a year sabbatical from the pack to teach me the basics and make sure I wasn't going to go crazy being a werewolf.

Kilkari and Harris came in with their arms loaded with bags and camping gear.

"You look like you're moving in, Cin." Harris deposited his pile near the front windows.

"You've got more things here than Vash and I do." I couldn't help but chuckle.

"A girl's got to be comfortable." Cin cocked her head and pointed to the pile of gear. "This is enough for two girls, which is what we are, aren't we, Vash?"

Vash stood next to her and mirrored her stance perhaps a little too well. "We are."

We all laughed. Even devoid of real furniture and trappings, the place was already feeling like a real home.

"We need to get going." Kilkari turned back toward the door.

As Cin hurried over to say her goodbyes, I knelt and held out my arms to Vash.

She rushed over, leaving a little stream of excited sparks in her wake. Wrapping her arms around my neck, she hugged me tightly.

"You be good for Cin tonight, okay? I'll see you tomorrow." I returned her hug, then kissed the top of her head.

"I will. If you get into trouble, I'll be right there, but I'll tell Cin first." She sounded so serious.

"Okay. You do that." I let go of her and stood. I turned and looked at Cin as she stepped away from Kilkari. "If you two need anything."

"We'll be fine." She smiled. "Plus, I've got your card."

"That you do. Remember I like manly things. No

flowers in the main room and such."

She punched me in the shoulder. "I think I've got your number, Lucas. Take care of Chad for me."

"I will." We weren't taking any camping gear with us. What was the point if we were just going to get naked and run in fur?

Minutes later, Kilkari pulled down my driveway and headed toward the street. I glanced back. Vash stood on the porch waving with sparks dancing around her and our friends at her side. It was nice knowing I'd be coming home to a real home the next day.

Lucas and Vash's story continues soon in "Flame"

As Lucas tries to adjust to his new life as a werewolf and father to Vash, he's still struggling to understand all the ins and outs of the supernatural world. When Gavin Harris asks for Vash's help in tracking down some strange magics, they stumble on more than they expect and get swept away to Faerie. Even with Vash's djinn magic, will they have enough to get them out before they're eaten by dragons or worse? There are some things even Army Ranger training can't prepare a soldier for.

For some added scenes, including the werewolf attack on Lucas' unit, and how Vash became bonded to her bell, sign up for my newsletter.

A.M. Burns Bio:

A.M. Burns lives in the Colorado Rockies with his partner, several dogs, cats, horses, and birds. When he's not writing, he's often fixing fences, splitting wood, hiking in the mountains, or flying his hawks. He's enjoyed writing since he was in high school, but it wasn't until the past few years that's he's begun truly honing his craft. He is a previous president of the Colorado Springs Fiction Writers Group. www.csfwg.org. Having lived both in Colorado and Texas, rugged frontier types and independent attitudes often show up in his work. You can find out more about A.M. and his writing at www.amburns.com .

Social media links.

Website: www.amburns.com
Email : andy@amburns.com
Facebook:
www.facebook.com/authoramburns
Goodreads author page:
http://www.goodreads.com/author/show/513
4598.A_M_Burns
Amazon Author Page:
http://www.amazon.com/-/e/B0054EVI6W
Mystichawker Press Author Page:
http://www.mystichawker.com/amburns.html
Colorado Springs Fiction Writers Group
http://www.csfwg.org

Other Books by A.M. Burns

Shifter Force
1: Visions of Rage
2: Visions of Shadows
3: Visions of Stars

Yellow Sky Coven:
1: Blood Moon Yellow Sky
2: Dark Stars of Dallas

Stand Alone Books:
The Black Fin Case

YA Books:
Coyote's Pup

Familiar Series:
1: Familiar Path
2: Familiar Spirit

Books in the Infragilis Universe.

Solstice Properties Mysteries
1: Second Story Hex
2: Watchtower WooWoo
3: Mid-Century Monster

Tempest Academy Prologue
Running in a Pack
Into the Sky
Shifting Tides

Want to see the story behind Cin Kilkari's first encounter with Agent Briar and learn more about what life is like raising two witch daughters and dealing with the ghost of her mother, Be sure to check out the Solstice Properties Mysteries.

The Stone place.

It started out as just another house to renovate for Cin and Chad Kilkari. Of course, the skeletons in the backyard were just the start of major complications.

Magic and house flipping collide. Can the duo fix the house and save Cottonwood, Colorado from the dark magic buried there?

If you like snarky witches and charming werewolves, with a Southwest flavor, you can't miss this new cozy series. It's sure to keep you up all night until the last page that leaves you thirsting for more.

Don't wait, buy Second Story Hex today!
Available at your favorite bookstore.

Visions
of
Rage
SHIFTER FORCE
BOOK 1
A.M. Burns
&
A.T. Weaver

Blood runs deep in Jemez Springs.

Psychic cougar shifter Connor McGriffin is used to his visions leading him around. For years, he's followed them back and forth across the country to the people who need his help. When his comfortable vacation in the mountains is interrupted by a vision of a woman dying, he can't see enough details to find the killer and stop him from striking again. Facing the most dangerous foe he's ever dealt with, Connor needs all the help he can get.

Small town deputy and wolf shifter, Danny Lupan is getting bored of chasing speeders and the occasional drug dealer. When the call comes that Sandoval County has its first murder in years, and it happened in his jurisdiction, he jumps at the chance to find the killer, no matter the danger involved. Little does he know, he might lose his heart, his life, or maybe both.

When a cougar and a wolf join forces, the bad guys better watch out, because the fur's going to fly, in more ways than one.

Join Connor and Danny on their first adventure together in the start of the fast-paced, suspenseful thriller series Shifter Force.

Available at your favorite bookstore.

Blood Moon
Yellow Sky
Yellow Sky Coven Book 1
A.M. Burns

A war is about to break out, and the combatants are who everyone expects. Can a dragon and a young mage stand in the middle of it and hope to get out alive?

Tal O'Duirwood, druid dragon, enjoys his quiet life of solitude in the Colorado mountains. When the need arises, Tal is the one the Coalition of Magical Creatures calls on to handle problems no one else can. For years he's worked on his reputation as the thing of nightmares for those who step out of the shadows. He never realized what was missing from his life until his gets an assignment to travel to Yellow Sky, Texas and help a witch and her students there stop a vampire invasion. Once there, he finds things were not as he was told. The witch is actually a werecoyote, and one of her students has eyes for Tal. Can Tal help stop the vampires in time to save his blossoming love? Will his heart, so long closed off from the world, be able to open to the touch of the handsome young mage

Available at your favorite bookstore.

The
Black
Fin
Case
A.T. Weaver
&
A.M. Burns

For several months, Detective Greg Williams and his partner have been trying to catch the Black Fin gang. Their latest intelligence is good, so they go on their most risky raid yet. But things go horribly wrong. While recuperating from the wounds he received during the botched raid, Detective Williams and his captain realize there might be a leak in the Portland police department. When they begin digging, things get worse for Williams.

At the urging of his captain, Detective Williams heads into the mountains, hoping a little distance from the department will give the Black Fins and their police informants the opportunity to slip up. His working vacation soon takes turns he could never have imagined when he meets the reclusive writer, Ken Draiag, next door, who turns out to be more than Greg ever imagined. But the Black Fins aren't about to let Detective Williams rest, they soon track him down, but with Ken's help, Greg manages to stay alive and fight back as forces he never knew existed reveal themselves to be working against him. Will Greg survive the Black Fins' ultimate plot?

Available at your favorite bookstore.